BUTTERFLY
and
SERPENT

A Novel by
Michael Robbins

Published by
    Vainglorious Press
        papablues050164@gmail.com

ISBN: 978-0-692-09210-1

First edition

Printed in the United States of America

CONTENTS

DEDICATION

—To my grandmother Elsy—
who always had faith in my writing.

—And to my brother Kenny—
though small in stature
he was always larger than life;
wish you were here, bro.

SHWARI (CALM)

SWEAT PASTED THE INTERVIEWER'S HAND to his notepad. In this gilded age at least, flies presented little problem since the anuran statutes at every table eradicated the pests with precision-targeted bolts of static energy.

Across from him, the woman stirred her mint tea with her fingertip, inciting a mild whirlpool in the murky green liquid. The umbrella shielding them cast shadowy streaks across her gorgeous brown complexion.

Their association had been a long one, characterized by an extended period of trust building. His editors couldn't press him hard enough for the most intimate details of her adult lifestyle, few of which were forthcoming. It had been those details that had dispatched him over the seas in the first place.

Rumor and tidbits carried on the East African Global network suggested a juicy story to his editors. Assuming the subject was willing — and she had been — re: the many incidents relative to her childhood. As their collaboration inched towards her teen years, his expectation of a major scoop mounted.

Yet, his instincts screamed that she'd been holding back, either subconsciously or deliberately. He nearly slapped the table in triumph when her remarks confirmed his belief.

"I think," she spoke, whispered almost with a huskiness that drew the interviewer into an adoring spell. "I think," she repeated, "there are certain facts that I can now trust you with."

Oh-ho, after a fifteen-year association, he should hope so, and said as much to the lady. She could chortle now, an outcome not evident from what she'd told him of her travels.

"The things I must tell you are deeply personal," she said as she continued to stir her tea leaves. "To be honest, it is difficult to slide back into that old skin… uncomfortable, to remember the person that I was. But my therapist, Celeste, feels that I'm now ready."

His next thought was that if she planned on peppering her dialogue with the usual load of Swahili euphemisms, he'd be obliged to compile a glossary and a brief sketch of the characters involved, such as they usually have in old Russian novels.

"I doubt our story is going to be that discombobulated," she laughed, but agreed that the inclusion of those two items at the end of his manuscript, would be a considerate gesture toward his readers.

Right, he thought. *Note to self to that effect. And was she also going to explain that crap with the snakes, as she'd promised?*

That elicited a sharp glare, painful as well as discomfited. "That will come in time. One has to… well, I had to be certain you'd accept the ordinary facets of my youth before entrusting the more bizarre details to print."

More? This story gets even stranger?

A smile, wise beyond her years, creased her full, rich mouth. "You have no idea," she replied.

The interviewer dabbed his brow, then scrubbed furiously at hands that seemed to drip in spite of the mildly temperate afternoon. During the following weeks and before too many notepads were filled, he believed the perspiration would never stop.

WOMB

MY FIRST MEMORIES WERE OF WATER, all warm and clingy, and a steady thrum-thrum as of a drum. I also remember a song whispered by an angel. What the words were, I couldn't recall, other than one which was repeated over and over: e-ay-as. No, that wasn't exactly what it was. Time blurs all things.

I was torn from this snuggly cocoon into a world of insects and light, screeching birds and shrieking winds. But again that angel trilled a song for my ears alone, and the word would come: e-ay-as, e-ay-as.

Mama died shortly after my delivery. I'd never seen her face. In my infant memory it's fuzzy and shadowed, but the song she whispered in the womb and at my birth remains in my mind. On those nights when I lie in Nyoka's embrace I call her voice to mind, and I can pretend it is Mama keeping me safe.

As for that word, I could never find what it meant, not from my father Baba (who vehemently denied all knowledge of it) nor from the East African Community's database, surely the greatest accumulation of facts in all the world. I only discovered the truth about this and many other things on that day when the spirits led me to the temple.

TEMPLE

(Based on interviews with Jamai Fatima Dlamini)

THIS WAS NOT HOW I INTENDED TO SPEND THIS EVENING. I'd been running all afternoon trying to escape the shade at my back. Several times I wished that Ngai would gaze down from Kere-Nyaga and have mercy on his wayward daughter. Just as I thought I could go no farther, I stumbled onto a moss-covered staircase set in a broad clearing.

This I found peculiar. I advanced to the top step.

The words engraved in the marble block to my right and at my feet indicated that this building had been dedicated in the year 2025, about 500 years before I was born. That would explain the dense liana obscuring the entry, as well as the words, a form of Old Swahili. Below the lettering was a curious symbol showing two hands, palms turned upward, with seven candle flames arising from their tips.

On the threshold, I hesitated. I had seen many a ruin dating from the Lost Age on school trips. So many records had been lost during the final wars of the 21st Century, where EMF pulses gone mad had erased the amassed information of the Western powers, it's hard to separate truth from prevailing wisdom. Yet I knew this one was different. An overpowering sense of majesty flared through my marrow. I didn't feel worthy to enter.

I was still huddled there, hands clutched to my mouth, when a swarm of butterflies — my totem — fluttered from inside. They came in many colors; blue, gray, or chalk-white, some with two tails trailing from their hind wings. Then there was the chestnut fellow with black margins and white dots who breezed about my cheeks.

Tiny feet pressed to my shoulders. The invitation seemed clear. I raised my hand towards the coarse tangle of gekonyi vines and creepers. With a loud rustle, they parted and I slipped inside.

That old familiar blackout swept over me even before I'd passed through the curtain of vines. Once I was clear, I reached for the medicinal gourd on my sash.

My doctor, S'manga Nlebela, believes that my cells produce a hormone to protect me from the energy I absorb to utilize my power. Excess amounts of this hormone tend to dissolve my blood's potassium ions, which explained the exhaustion that overcomes me every time I make an outburst. S'manga has prescribed this medicine to restore these lost electrolytes since I was twelve years old.

I took a deep swallow as the foliage shuttered me in darkness, and my face screwed into the usual furrows. Three years of sipping it and the stuff still tasted bitter, sickly-sour. But you cannot cure a bad ill with sweet medicine. I called out, "Lights!"

Nothing happened. Ah, I know. This ruin was built before voice-controlled appliances were widespread in our country. I inched forward, groping at air… until the floor dropped away!

I crashed onto a flat-topped surface, which collapsed and pitched me to a tiled floor. The gourd rolled into the shadows as a musty cloth draped me. I lay sprawled, arms and legs throbbing, before I threw off the cloth. I had to have that gourd!

I scrambled about the floor, brushing aside bowls and corroded utensils and dust balls. From nowhere and everywhere came a constant drip-drip of water.

What had happened here? I never knew of such a place near Baba Elgonyi, my home village. Ceramic fragments poked at my soft-soled boots. A missile, then. That would fit the times. This house may have been targeted by rival warlords, or blown up by accident. Whatever the cause, it was sad to see it in such a state.

A cloying presence swelled in my belly. Ngai, no! Dust billowed from a side passage. Damn it, I shouldn't even be here; I was supposed to be home studying history with Youssou. My fingers abruptly closed on the gourd. I ducked behind a heap of rubble and held my breath. He glided in soon after.

No face appeared behind his gray shroud, only two orange balls. An upper sleeve might vanish under a shaft of light, only to reappear once he slunk into shadow. A savage wind preceded him, fanning in every direction. Our storytellers say that those spirits who die in sin become ogres full of malice. This one was like a *morathi wa nauma*, a seer of darkness. My hands wouldn't stop shaking as he called out. "*Toto*…child, where are you? I bear you no ill will, but this sanctuary must be protected. Come forth, I shall be just."

He repeated this call several times, like a voice from the pit. Finally he was gone. I let a stale breath go with a gasp and pushed on down a side corridor.

MY FATHER? OH, BABA IS A GREAT MAN. He serves as Executive Horticulturalist for the Sahara Reclamation Project, a multigenerational plan to re-green the desert. Baba could be onsite for the project for weeks at a time when I was a small *toto*. Grandmother would always be the one to nanny me. We couldn't trust anyone else.

It goes back to the strange incidents at the Harvest Festival ten years ago. I'd only just turned five. That had been the first inkling that I might be different. Sometimes I'm not sure that I hadn't imagined it all. But the scars on my thighs say it was so.

That season's festival was to celebrate the 300th anniversary of the end of the genocidal wars, to remember the price we had paid in blood and disease to discover our common brotherhood. I hadn't been permitted to go; the pretext then was that I was too young. Yet if that was so, why had the other village children been allowed to accompany their parents?

My chief tormentor, Nyassa, had been detailed to be my sitter that night, probably as a punishment for her constantly calling me bad names. Her friends had crept back to our village after the adults had departed for the celebrations at our neighboring village of Kibarenge. They persuaded Nyassa to abandon me so she could join the festivities.

That wasn't the worst part by far. I believe I've mentioned in previous conversations the colossal statue of the Ant Totem that once stood proud facing the Communal House in the village square of Baba Elgonyi. Well, the reason that statue no longer shadows our homes is because that statue attacked me.

No, no I'm quite serious. The entire structure pivoted down on its thorax and snatched my legs in its pincers. It surged back to its imposing height and shook me like a doll, gouging serrations deep into my hips and thighs. The thing tossed me into an anthill and laughed as I scrambled away. I dove into a mud wallow to scrub the ants off me.

But I hadn't been alone that chilly night. As the dew formed on my shaking limbs, my totem whispered to me for the first time. "Don't be afraid, little one," it said. "*Lala Salama.* Sleep. We shall watch over you in Nyassa's absence." Butterfly wings spread into a living blanket over my body.

Ahela, sister of my best friend Youssou, found me the next morning. Grandmother Cele carried my limp body to

Kibarenge where everyone could see what Nyassa's negligence had done to me. Nobody believed my story… not the important part. Not even *bibi* Cele. Baba saw to it that the statue was destroyed anyway.

Oh, I wish I could deny it'd ever happened. But you can't deny the evidence when it's gouged into your living flesh. I don't know what power animated the statue that night. I don't suppose it mattered, not in present circumstances.

If only Youssou could see this place. He's earned high enough marks in Upper School to graduate early, and was already reviewing visual proposals from several universities. Old architecture is one of his interests. I bet he'd be in the clouds if he could study this house.

I don't know why, it just seemed proper to call it a house. The floors creaked on some levels, while others were blocked by rubble. Time had blackened murals that had crumbled to the tile. Everywhere dust clung thick to my fingertips.

That symbol of candles-in-palms was emblazoned on several supports. In certain passages this was overlaid by another symbol, seared clumsily over the first. That one showed a woman with waist-length hair spreading her arms in supplication. I didn't understand what this overlapping of symbols meant. Anyhow, I had greater worries.

As I descended an ancient metal escalator, my thoughts returned to that afternoon. Alone in the forest I'd focused my will at rocks and trees, visualizing them dancing in the air. Instead, stone cracked as if from hammer blows. Trees uprooted themselves, spraying rust-tinted dirt a dozen meters wide. I balled my fists and frowned. Of course it wasn't going to be easy, but…

I'd had this power, this *curse* since my seventh rain. It'd grown bits at a time over the intervening years. I could do so many things just by wishing for it to be so. But I didn't have the power to make people like me.

The people of Baba Elgonyi held a deeply rooted conceit that they were the true custodians of African tradition. As part of that conceit they bore a bitter distrust of anyone who differed from the norm. And I was different, very much so. Certainly, I was taller by a head than the other girls in my age grade. My hair, though naturally wavy, lacked a peppercorn curl. No, it hung straight down to my waist. My skin was lighter than what was considered normal, more of a copper shade than brown.

If it had only been those things, I might have overcome their prejudice. The power complicates things. It made people afraid.

Often I'd wonder as the teen years approached whether this power could have been hereditary, whether it had been passed down to me through my mother's line. Baba usually skirted this issue with a terse "mmmph", feigning increased interest in his irrigation graphs and whatever results pertained to that.

Two years ago, while we camped under the stars on the Masai Mara plains, I thought I'd had him pinned. But rather than push me away as the subject always drove him to, he cuddled me closer with only our blankets between us.

"It's possible," he'd admitted. "We hadn't been married long. If we'd had more time together, perhaps I could say." He flicked a glance my way and added, "You seem to have inherited her mischievous streak at least."

An overwhelming surge choked in my throat, accompanied by an empathic wave of despair. My forehead got clammy. A few moments passed and Baba had quelled the sadness he was hiding from me. I hadn't the courage to press him for more details, not then or since.

When I told these things to S'manga Nlebela, who also acted as my part-time advisor, he suggested that the sensible course would be to master this power. This made perfect sense, so I replied, "I accept your challenge, oh wise mondo-mogo."

That was why I skipped school to fly to this deserted glade five kilometers from home. No one today understands the power of our ancestral spirits. The Old Ways were lost in the chaos following the genocidal wars. I would have to train myself. Smanga offered a few suggestions: that I must strive for a state of calm, then visualize in my mind what the desired effect should be. All well and good. Now if I could just lift those rocks instead of making them burst…

Suddenly the earth swelled beneath me. Roots twisted around both my ankles. I yelped as they tightened, gouging into my flesh. An icy breeze blew through me, and there stood the Morathi, shimmering in the midday light. I was too astonished to speak. But he had no such inhibitions.

"Hear me, *toto*," he intoned. "I have watched you and those like you since the earliest manifestation of your power. And I remember what your brethren did to our temple."

My… what was he jabbering about? I tugged at my ankle, but the roots jerked me back to my knees. The Morathi wagged a gloved finger, which phased in and out of existence. "It is plain by what I have seen this day that you have grown too unstable to allow free roam. In the name of Elias, I must destroy you."

I should have been frightened when his digits crackled with energy. But this was the final indignity. The only reason people harassed me was because I was different! That wasn't my fault. Who was this towel headed ogre to judge me?

Still on hands and knees, I shouted, "I'll show you power!" I slapped my elbows to my sides. Dirt geysered in a crimson shower that swallowed him whole. The roots loosened and I sprang free. Then I was running, tumbling I knew not where. Deeper and deeper I charged into the forest until I came to this ruin.

A furious bellow rocked me to my knees. A chunk of marble smashed into my stomach. The walls rushed past me in a blur, and I landed a dozen meters away in a livid rage. As the Morathi advanced through a red haze, I focused my attention on the roof.

A coffin-sized section groaned and buckled. Debris rumbled down in a dry waterfall between us. I couldn't see him. Good. That'd buy me some rest time. Yes... eyelids weighing so heavily...

A stench of flaming ash aroused me. My eyes teared as I caught sight of three figures darting along this... immaculate corridor?

It was the same, but not. Walls glistened. The carpet was plush beneath my belly; it even smelled of wildflowers. The people seemed to be in quite a state, their arms loaded with discs. Their uniforms were all vest-coats and breeches. A basso-voiced fellow cried, "Brother Esaias is dead... or worse. I don't know what's happened to him."

Fireballs rattled the air like Ngai's footsteps, spraying and pinging and shrieking in my ears. Aii! When would it end? I buried my face in my arms and screamed.

Then it stopped. Dirt sifted down from the top of the barrier I'd just yanked down. The walls had returned to their fallen state. Besides that, three new players now bent over me. The running figures.

Words can't convey the beauty of their shining faces. All beckoned with open hands. The curly haired Caucasian female with them bent over me and smiled. "We've been waiting a long time for you, daughter."

Strange, how quickly everything turned…

"…Jamai…"

I rose on aching limbs. Shivers rattled my bones at this call. Had those three visages returned? No, nobody was about. The voice called again, like a whisper of wind through the kopjes where the lions once sunned. Had I heard these words before, in spirit?

"I… I'm here," I said.

Warmth soothed me from the inside out. Yes, the spirit of my totem was very near. "We are here," it said. "Fear not."

"Why haven't you spoken before? I needed you." Actually, my totem never spoke, not since it comforted me on that long-ago night after the ants attacked me, the night it had chosen Ahela and me. "Tell me why I'm here," I pleaded.

The spirit replied in a gentle matron's voice. "The need has not been as great before. We have a purpose in leading you hither, child. Come… follow."

I scrambled over rubble as my totem led me deeper into this house, calling, "Follow, follow!" The damage wasn't as extensive in this wing. Everything would be fine now; my friend was here. Doors that were never automated opened at my approach, as though thrust aside by invisible hands.

We arrived in a library stocked full of information discs. People used to say those things were indestructible, but they say that about everything. On we went, weaving past shelves to a primitive type of workstation. This had been reduced to a semi-circular charred lump. In some way it brought back memories of the desktop in Ahela's kitchen where we'd loaded funny pictures into her mother's recipe files.

On top of the station sat a crystalline cube jammed full of microcircuits. I recognized it from our Roots of Technology class as a kinetic-sensor recorder. All that was needed to start it was the warmth of a human hand. A disc was still lodged in the PLAY slot. Could it still work after all these rains?

"Is this why I was called?" I asked.

"Touch it, child. Listen."

I did as directed. The disc whirred. Then, in front of the station appeared the image of a man that reminded me of my father. It said, "Brethren, my name is Esaias Pahoran Dlamini..."

My heartbeat quickened. He had my name!

"...steward to the Ancient Order of Elias for this African outpost. I stood watch, as do you on the earth's other continents, for the day when our fallen sister Sydelle rises again."

That was the second time I'd heard the name Elias since this misadventure began. What connection did he have with my ancient grandfather, or the evil shade hounding me? Where did this fallen sister Sydelle fit in the puzzle?

These questions faded as I viewed my ancestor. I'd never seen such outlandish garments, even in old stills from our histories. The neckline of his top garment was tucked up to his chin. His waistcoat was a pleasant dark shade of blue with the collar flaps turned wide.

What a beautiful man he must have been. I sensed a gentle disposition in his soft-spoken tones and sparkling eyes. I wish I could have known him.

The account continued. "Since Mombasa became an inland delta because of the rising seas, a mass of refugees fled into the interior. Several political factions have drawn followers from these masses. The most prominent among these are the Constitution Party and the Morani Republicans.

"The single belief uniting this pair is that only by a return to traditional ways can we hope to survive. To that end they intend to found a new home, a Baba Elgonyi, after the Masai holy mountain. This is a flawed assumption. Our customs have been forever altered since contact with white men in colonial times. What has been done cannot be undone."

I shifted position as he paused to dab his brow. I'd heard of these factions in school, but only as names and usually in glowing terms. Now I was learning from a voice out of the dust.

"…It was over implementation of their ideals that the Freemen and Morani have come to arms. Their fighting was waged across mountain and scrub until it arrived at our doorstep.

"A mother and her two sons came to this outpost seeking sanctuary. I had my son Benjamin conduct them to a chapel five kilometers to the east. Not surprisingly…" Here Grandfather sighed, rubbing a hand to his brow. "…a Morani Republican came looking for them.

"Evidently this family fled a Morani camp to escape the fighting. This act branded them as a nest of spies. Since they had come to me, well, it was clear that not only was our order in league with them but with the government as well. It is an old suspicion, and one not likely to change.

"There was no reasoning with this Morani, a Lord Spencer Molefe, though I used all my powers of persuasion in the attempt. Failing that, and with no real government forces to call on for aid, I was forced into a technological solution."

The image tapped his earlobe where a crude microelectric device was clearly evident. "One of my gifts is a sensitivity to electromagnetic fields. My cells possess hormonal compounds which protect me from such fields."

"O Holy Ngai," I whispered. "Just as I do."

"Years of study under Professor Elias have enabled me to control this energy, even to draw it into cohesive patterns for brief periods. My brethren have established a rudimentary datalink between myself and our in-house computer, which has greatly enhanced my abilities. By projecting images of creatures from folklore, such as monsters made from sticks, or a man with a great blue ox, we had hoped to use the Moranis' own beliefs against them." Grandfather's hands rose and fell, slapping sharply against his thighs. "Our tactics have been only marginally success…"

Grandfather glanced sidewise, and his eyes grew as wide as drumheads. For the first time his composure cracked. "Power generation is erratic. They're trying to sabotage our lines to the regional power grid. I'll have to download…"

As he reached for his earpiece, the image flashed. Grandfather's mouth yawned in a soundless shriek. A wicked aura framed his body as his features darkened. He became a silhouette, his eyes glowing like fireballs.

I slapped my hand to my mouth. I didn't see that!

The library doors exploded off their hinges. I bolted for the hall, my eyes burning with tears. Finally I burst into another chamber. Crashing to the floor, I lay wheezing.

I'd learned at my father's knee that the Morani and Republicans engaged in several titanic — and futile — battles. Then Benjamin Dlamini, the greatest of my ancestors, came as a man out of the wilderness. It was he, Baba said, the son of Esaias Dlamini, who became the father of Baba Elgonyi.

Those who followed Benjamin Dlamini said it was our foolishness that had swept so much of Mother Earth into the dung heaps, and ourselves nearly as well. If this great venture was to succeed, they said, we must be as industrious as the ant. See how Ngai's smallest creatures can erect such huge natural edifices as their great anthills.

By unanimous vote, the first Council of Elders of our village adopted the ant, first as an inspiration to the disillusioned youth of that time. In succeeding generations, it evolved into a totem unto itself, until the night that I was attacked.

Until my birth, my family had been the most respected in the district. Until now, no one knew what had become of Benjamin's father. Ngai forgive me, I wish I didn't.

A wisp of air brushed my shoulders, like the touch of butterfly wings. "Child," my totem called, "why do you run?"

I couldn't look up. "Why do you tell me these things? I... I thought you were my friend. That thing can't be my grandfather."

"We tell you these things so you may understand. You mustn't fear, for he believes he serves Father Ngai, even as we do."

"I don't...?"

"Ngai sent us to guide you on the right path. You are one of Ngai's special ones, Jamai Fatima, and you were given power for a special task, which we cannot reveal to you." She paused. "Didn't you know this?"

I shook my head as I scooted onto my knees. "B... but Grandfather..."

"Esaias Dlamini's spirit was inextricably linked to these grounds. His determination, combined with the uplink which enhanced his consciousness, acted together to transform his essence into the imperfect being you have seen."

"I'm only fifteen. What can I do?"

"Search your heart, child. Bask in the peace that surrounds you. We will tell you what to say when the time comes."

And then my totem was silent. I knelt alone on the dusty floor. Yes, it was a quiet place. The benches had crumbled to rot ages ago. The light fixtures hung useless. Ash coated the surface of every wall canvass, but if I could dust them off…

I tore a strip from the *kanga* wrap bound to my waist and set to work. The image was damaged by oxidation, but it seemed to represent a tall Euro in a sand-colored suit surrounded by happy *totos*. His expression was wise and grandfatherly. Given what order this house subscribed to, there wasn't much doubt about who he was.

"Jambo, Elias," I said. "Were you as wise as your image tells me you were?" I skipped to the next canvas.

Activity is an excellent cleanser of the spirit. While I scrubbed, it occurred to me that in spite of my recent frights, this Morathi was still my grandfather. He had been lost from our ancestral roots; I suppose I had an obligation to recover him.

I had no right to even contemplate what I was about to do. Such ceremonies were the province of Elders and seers. It would also require participation of the entire family group. According to tradition, no individual could propitiate the spirits.

What family did I have? Uncle Kadar's clan had never accepted me, apart from Grandmother Cele. As head of the family, Baba should officiate this proceeding. But he wasn't as steeped in tradition as I was. He was a horticultural biologist who understood me in terms of biochemistry and physics. Matters of the spirit would not interest him.

Besides, our Elders were learned men, learned in the ways of the world. In this age, they relied on information protocols. The advice of seers would more likely be received with ridicule than favor, even if I knew one. No, this would have to be up to me.

Having decided, I spread my improvised dust cloth on a jade podium and knelt on the floor. I fished a pair of incense sticks from my waist pouch and broke them into four pieces, casting them as lots on the floor.

Sometimes the power obeys my will, oftentimes not. This time when I stared at the shattered incense, they burst into flame. A sweet cinnamon scent soon wafted through the chamber. As I wished.

What else could I offer to appease the spirits? If they were flesh and blood, what would I offer them? My hands seemed to act of their own will, because as I was thinking this, they slipped the medicinal gourd from my kanga. "Father Ngai, why am I doing this?" I gulped, then rubbed a knuckle into my sore eyes.

I began again. "Reverend Elder, to whom the mountains bow and the clouds yield their rain, your unworthy child entreats you with this offering of the medicine that sustains her. Guide us so that we may welcome our fallen ancestor back into the fold. Let this child be your voice to our grandfather Esaias. Peace, we beseech you, o Ngai." I raised the gourd high and poured a libation onto the tiles.

It was at this task that the Morathi found me. Benches scattered like twigs in a typhoon. He swept his robe about him, bellowing, "We cannot abide darkness! I guard the way and the truth and the light!"

I rose and strode briskly along the bare floor. The time alone had strengthened me. I knew who he was and I wasn't afraid. Whatever else he had to say, I silenced with a hard slap across the hood.

For a spirit, he gave my hand a substantial sting. His glowing orbs shrunk to pinpricks of surprise. "How dare you defile this house! Is this how you served Professor Elias, by promising death to all those you meet? How dare you spit in Elias' face?"

A breeze wafted through his shroud. He pivoted to one side, perhaps to consider my words. "Grandfather," I said, "look at me."

He regarded me with eyes of fire. I flinched, but then, squaring my shoulders, I took his hand and pressed it to my temple. Scientists say our thoughts are only loosely organized particles of charged energy. If this Morathi could interface with a 21st Century database, he could do as much to my mind.

Words flowed from my tongue, just as my totem promised. "I know you were Esaias Dlamini in another life. Your son Benjamin brought my people peace and founded our village, Baba Elgonyi. I am your granddaughter, and the spirits have sent me to help…"

When his other hand clasped my chin, all the boldness suddenly drained out of me. What was I thinking? What had the spirits talked me into? His clammy cloak now engulfed me like a shroud. I tried to twist free of that moldering cloth. It enfolded, chafed, but held me tight.

Grandfather's twin fireballs bore into my consciousness. My stomach churned as his thoughts invaded mine, punching through my defenses as if they didn't exist. Pain spiked through my skull, but I wouldn't panic. He had to see I wasn't a threat.

What's worse was that at every level he penetrated, I relived all the horrors of my short life. The time Nyassa and I were buried alive, chasing a Nightcrawler into its den. The day the children dunged me on the Masai Mara plains. The night that Mama died.

Then, the blinding glare dimmed. Sparkling hazel eyes gazed into mine, as moistened by tears as my own. The pressure on my skull lessened.

As his mind withdrew, I relived Grandfather's misery, too: the anxiety of a father not knowing whether his son escaped the Morani alive. The despair of seeing all that he cherished fail.

The fear of being trapped in a shell he could never escape, in a ruin he'd failed to protect and might never leave.

"We're not so different, are we, Grandfather?" I wheezed.

Grandfather deposited me on my feet. I wobbled on shaky legs as he "sat" in the air, where I suppose a bench had been. "Benjamin prevailed," he said. "That is well. But when he was gone they followed their own degenerate impulses. How can I atone for what I've done, child?"

My eyeballs still throbbed from his probing. I rested my hand on his shoulder. It yielded like a cloth-covered bladder. "You have seen the record?"

"I have."

He swirled around to clasp my hands, gently but firmly. "No one must know of this place. If the Children of Sydelle were to find this outpost… promise me this."

"No one will know, Grandfather." I crouched at his knees. It seemed clear for what purpose the spirits had guided me here. "Grandfather, teach me. Show me how to control the power I've been given."

"Elias would wish this."

"Was he a wise man?"

"Oh yes, the wisest, kindest man on seven continents. He united us for a wise purpose."

"Does this involve your fallen sister Sydelle? Is it her symbol which defaces your own?" Sitting this near him, I had perceived the candle-in-palms mark stitched on either side of Grandfather's hood.

For a heartbeat he faded from view like a shadow blending into the dark. Then he reappeared. "My memory has many gaps. She was one of us, once. But you are perceptive, child. That is her brand. I recall little else."

"Is that the price you ask for your wisdom?" My fingers clutched at his knees. "Our databases are huge. Even a child such as I could find what you need."

Grandfather swelled to his feet. "I know you will find the truth. Come again in two nights… after school," said he, wagging his finger. "Summon me when you are ready to leave. I'll show you a quicker way out."

I rested my head on his shoulder, this spirit that had once been my ancestor. His arms encircled me as a cool evening mist. Then he vanished through a wall, as soft as a cloud.

I remained kneeling before a canvas of Elias and his stewards. And for that brief space of time, my spirit knew peace.

ASIDES: THE WARS

Recollections of Jamai Fatima Dlamini

TELL YOU OF THE FUTURE? Am I now some kind of seer? (laughs) Where would you have me begin? Well, I can give you a broad outline. History always was one of my favorite subjects in school. The problem lies in the fact that much of it is lost-- literally.

You must understand that by the phrase "Lost Age", we're not simply referring to the genocidal wars of your time…oh don't deny it! Your Balkan tribes and yes, even my own kin, have been practicing mass murder for ages, while the so-called Superpowers either played us off each other for their own ends, or worse, stood to one side and did nothing.

The polar ice caps melted, another sin of your negligence. Besides exposing the true minuscularity of Antarctica, the rising seas swallowed whole island chains, coastlines on every inhabited continent. Uncounted thousands were forced inland, in places such as India, China and Hispanic America, over lands already severely overpopulated. The nuclear exchanges to come were only a desperate reflection of the insanity we'd brought on ourselves.

This much is known, the first exchange was actually a coordinated attack on the Levant, the land between the Turkish peninsula and the Fertile Crescent. It's never been established exactly who those powers were, though the American Union and the Chinese were always prime suspects. Does it matter now who did it? It was hardly a secret that the two major sects inhabiting the region were never going to come to peace. "God" gave them this land, they said, and both had a legitimate claim to it.

Some conservative elements believe bombing the Levant to radioactive atoms was the best thing that'd ever happened to this planet. I don't know about that. The whole affair seems ridiculous now, killing themselves by degrees over a narrow strip of land barely 400 km. long by 200 km. across.

This is why it was a mistake: prior to this incident, the nuclear-bearing nations had operated under a principal of mutually imposed restraint with regard to these weapons. After that single eleven-minute exchange, all bets, as you'd say, were off.

Europe was surprisingly spared by the larger nuclear firestorm. By that time Euro's sons had fewer ongoing internal conflicts, certainly none bordering on the homicidal. Still, those exchanges were the final nail in the fall of the entity known as the "nation-state". What we know of this has been largely passed down by word of mouth. It had to be.

You see, much of our world's data had been converted to digital streaming. And all of that was lost in the electro-magnetic pulses resulting from the nuclear exchanges, along with the information physically contained in books. It wasn't so catastrophic as the dearth of knowledge that characterized your medieval period, but it was hard enough. But the best was yet to come…

LETTER TO THE ENEMY

MY BELOVED ACOLYTE,

Allow us first to extend this opportunity for you to assume our place in leading this exalted branch in service to our Mistress Sydelle. We know from your service to the Rheinland Branch that you are prepared to offer your all to the cause, not excluding the presentment of your very life. Accept our gratitude, and welcome home. The brief that follows will detail the progress of our current objectives.

In April previous, we became aware of a certain party that had been conducting data searches via the East African Community database and had been doing so for some time. Said individual identified themselves as "Bug One". Between December and May, we have detected 25 hits related to Sydelle (subject) or Children of cf. Our contact in the relevant homelands confirms this is the Registered EAC account for the Lepidopteran, to wit the young Jamai.

Per instructions already settled upon, c. 21 October, our team proceeded to the Tana River. Given the assessments gleaned from our agent in Baba Elgonyi, it was assumed that acquisition of the Lepidopteran would require enlistment of a greater power.

The object of our desires did not easily yield to our sweeps. For eleven nights, we dealt with UV-mutated vines grasping at our ankles and limestone slabs which caused us to stumble. Success came the eve of 7 November. We encountered our quarry in Search grid 21 within a millet field servicing a village 500 km. SE of Mount Kenya.

His enlistment was not without loss, brave acolyte. Chissamo, Hashemi, and Takriti perished in the initial struggle. Their sacrifice enabled us to expose the creature to the Collector.

The effects were most satisfactory. After much howling, the matrix at the Collector's core absorbed a sufficient portion of his life force to control him. The brand of our Mistress was placed on his left breast, his limbs bound in chains of iron. Transport to the Mau Escarpment was rendered. There he received the following commands:

Find the Lepidopteran; initiate surveillance; make her one of us.

Upon his release, we proceeded N to Mount Elgon. It is our hope, once the Lepidopteran is secured, that she too may act as a conduit to the inhabitants of the Other World, much as our Mistress did before her incarceration by Elias.

We expect a worthy report soon. Love life and wisdom,

BA, Chief Authority, Dobra Damo Branch COS

KALILA MAJI

Interview: Part 1

(Based on interviews with Jamai Fatima Dlamini)

HER NAME WAS KALILA SOFINA MAJI MOLEFE, the youngest of Odu Molefe's four offspring. That is too much to remember so everyone calls her Kalila Maji.

That was the extent of my knowledge that afternoon that I'd gone to Mokoyo Springs. Muted sunlight dappled the boulders protruding from the spring bed. Tortoises and shrimp scrambled under fallen pear-tree logs as I approached.

These were the times I craved the most. As tepid and stuffy as the air could be on the surface, below was a different matter. The water's buoyancy liberated my spirit even as it cooled my skin. I could forget that stupid power here, imagine I was only a sixteen-year-old girl. Forget Elias and Sydelle…

My lessons with Grandfather Esaias had been going wonderfully these last nine months. Mostly our visits involved the learning of basic meditation exercises, deep-breathing techniques intended to clear one's thoughts of all extraneous details. It's becoming possible to allow the power to flow through me without actually draining me.

It hasn't always been easy to sneak away to his sanctuary either, despite the absence of any extracurricular activities in my school schedule. I wasn't bloody well welcome among the girls of my age grade.

I could expect four days of Upper School per week, eight hours daily. Grandfather had insisted I maintain my high scores. Baba, bless him, still covered expenses for Comparative

Belief Systems classes, despite his frequent absences from home. Together my studies entail a great deal of take-home work. Ha! That much they couldn't take from me.

I'd graduate from Upper School the rainy season following the coming one. Before that they'd have to let me take part in an initiation ceremony with the other girls of my age grade. That is our tradition; all the children born in a certain time period studied together, played, and passed into adulthood together. We'd all be sisters and full-fledged members of the community.

Yes, there was a great deal on my mind at this time. Control of my power has grown, but it's still crude, much as my knowledge of the Ancient Order of Elias is. Their title is a conceit as their order is neither religious nor all that ancient. Their opponents were my chief interest, and they seemed as elusive as meerkats. But I didn't want to think about them; I only wanted to swim.

A blue-and-black brooder having the face of a pugnacious Elder foraged in the mud. With it swam a cloud of tiny hatchlings. The fish didn't mind resting in my cupped hands, although its young darted for the shelter of its mouth.

Tingling in the base of my skull. Grandfather had shown me how to distinguish between the spirits of flora, fauna, and people. Escaping bubbles tickled my nostrils as I sorted through these empathic impressions.

Youth… impatience. Someone's coming. No, three someones. The buzzing became more insistent, but where could I hide? I could stay submerged for up to two minutes… well, maybe longer now with Grandfather's teaching. But I'd like to at least see who the intruders might be. Releasing the brooder, I surfaced amid a thicket of reeds as rank as rotten hen's eggs.

Three youngsters approached on a beaten trail leading from home. Noticing their gangly limbs, I could see a family resemblance. First came seventeen-year-old Hwenge Molefe, then his younger brother Mutu. Between them walked a meek creature no higher than their armpits, their sister Kalila.

There was none of their haughtiness in her steps. She inched forward as though an owl might cross her path. Her bright hazel eyes were round as she clung to her kin, her hair braided with turquoise, amber, and conches. A brilliant sheen illuminated her unblemished cocoa skin.

How could the Almighty have stuck her with this family? The Molefes had always shown me an animosity that I couldn't understand. Their father even sent his oldest daughter Nyassa to private school in Eritrea eight seasons ago, when she first showed signs of friendship towards me.

It probably hadn't endeared me to him that we both chased a Nightcrawler to its den. He should complain. That brute chewed a hole in my scalp, not Nyassa's. Baba says Odu Molefe's mistrust stems from Mama's being an outsider to our village. Also, Mzee Molefe is an Elder with much ambition, and what he couldn't get through ability, he strove for by guile. Sadly, I had to be a pawn in his machinations.

I hoped they would move on. Instead they stopped beside an old baobab that branched into a pair of forks a few meters up its trunk. Hwenge and Mutu bundled Kalila into a floatation vest they took from Mutu's rucksack and guided her to the water.

I'd have laughed if I weren't stuck in those slimy reeds. Her legs beat the water into froth but she wasn't going anywhere. Why hadn't they taught her to float first? What were they on about anyhow?

Then Hwenge smacked Mutu for some imagined offense. Words passed between them. As I fumed, a chill crept along my spine. Second by second, bioenergy tingled along every nerve, fired by my indignation. This was my pond. They could go anywhere to teach her. Why did I have to be the one who was always hiding? Why couldn't they just go away?

The baobab's left fork split from the bole with a sharp crack. Four meters of tree about twelve millimeters thick arched down to impale Mutu's rucksack. Leaves tinkled down as though to conceal the evidence. I gulped and slipped deeper into the reeds. I hadn't meant to…

Ngai curse me; subconsciously, I probably did. The power still obeyed whims as well as orders.

Kalila's brothers waded ashore, but there was no budging that tree. They glanced at each other, then at the spring. Perhaps now they'd leave. Wait… they spoke hurried words to Kalila as they ran up the trail towards our village. That left her alone at the spring. It also left her in my power.

Who would ever know? She was the daughter of my worst tormentor. I could make the mud rise from the bottom and engulf her. Yet all I did was watch as her thrashing took her into deeper waters. My heart drummed faster in sympathy with hers as her anxiety mounted.

Don't be afraid, I thought. You're safe in that vest. Cup your hands, stroke the water.

And she did.

I stifled a shout of praise… barely. Had she sensed…? No, I could gather empathic impressions but not probe people's minds. Certainly, she didn't have such talents.

Neither of us glimpsed a huge pale tube undulate along the spring bed. Bubbles torpedoed around it as the creature shot upward, whipping around Kalila's throat with a wet slap. We both shrieked, "Nightcrawler!"

I didn't think about what I did next. These gen-altered worms kill several children every year in the Mau district. This one entangled itself around Kalila's arms as its teeth savaged her vest. Luckily its thick padding was protecting her neck, but that wouldn't hold off the worm for long. I paddled to her at once and grabbed Nightcrawler behind its head.

It exploded into a frenzy; clearly the attacker wasn't expecting to be attacked. Two meters of blubbery flesh released Kalila and squirmed around my arms. Fine… I wasn't the best snake wrestler in Baba Elgonyi for nothing.

Kicking up my legs, I dove headfirst toward the bottom. Water gushed into my nostrils as I shoved Nightcrawler's snout into the spring bed. Its tail lashed my ribs with savage thumps. Silt spewed around its snout but my fingers dug into the folds of its neck, deeper and…

Nightcrawler suddenly wrenched free and whipped into a mass of reeds. When the silt had settled, I spied Kalila pawing at the surface. Tiny bubbles trickled from her vest. She couldn't swim. With her vest breached…

Her head had nearly submerged before I caught her beneath the armpits. As we broke the surface, we both gulped the crisp fresh air. A shudder rocked Kalila. She must have realized who was treading water for her. "Don't be afraid," I told her. "I won't hurt you."

Praise the Maker, her breathing became less hoarse, even steadier. At that moment, she probably didn't care if her rescuer was the fabled Lord Greystoke himself.

Once ashore I carried her like a child through thick grass and young palm fronds to a stand of figs for which the springs were named. I could have carried her for hours; her weight was that slight. Still, it seemed best to set her down. No tension gripped her shoulders as I draped my towel over her. She tugged at her lower lip and continued to stare.

A strident cry ripped through the silence. Kalila's brothers had returned. Judging by how they shook their fists, they weren't coming to offer their praises either. Those boys threw themselves at me like rabid lions. I reversed their grips, braced both feet, and shoved them on their behinds.

I'd practiced self-defense for many an hour with our school's Poppy Girl. That training now proved its worth. They tumbled like disjointed monkeys, but they wouldn't stay down. Mutu took a swing at me with a thorn branch… aii! It stung, and a dozen pimples of blood rose from that scratch.

Instinct seized control and through it the power. I assumed a defensive stance and thrust my hand into Mutu's chest. I never touched him. Nevertheless, his body shrieked across the clearing into a wall of thorn vines. Good, you stupid, insolent *fisi*…

Granite smashed into my skull. I had forgotten Hwenge. Bone crunched as my mind flashed with fire. I thought Kalila screamed, but couldn't be certain because everything went…

Do you ever dream of water?

I tried to wake up; I really did. Each time a sea of nausea swamped me. In the enclosing darkness lay comfort. That and patches of crystalline light. A brooding mass clutched my waist. I didn't know what it might be, but its presence offered a measure of strength as it buoyed my spirit upward.

I surfaced atop a mass of decomposing papyrus. A fleet of mosquitoes whined in tightening spirals. North, south, east, west, it made no difference. The quaking greenery spread as far as my blurry eyes could see. In places the papyrus might be four meters in length, a fact I was experiencing firsthand.

That I found myself up to the armpits in the Sudd, the largest stinking marsh in East Africa, wasn't a surprise. I've dreamed of the pyramids, sailing the American Union's mighty Mississippi, and scooting upside-down along a Martian geodome. No, that was supplied by the pirogue gliding from a hazy blue mist. A smile dimpled Elias' pale cheeks as he held out his hand.

I was struggling to get closer when a sultry voice chuckled, "Poor naïve child. It isn't mummery you need. I realized that long ago. Come this way."

Lost in swirling mist, statuesque Sydelle bobbed waist-high in the all-encompassing humus. Her palms curled in a come-hither gesture.

Elias beckoned. "This is the path of light, child."

Sydelle sang, "This is the path of belonging. Come."

Always I swirled from one to the other, both appealing, both out of reach. Twice more in my dreams I returned to that imaginary Sudd. Neither time could I choose between the paths they represented. In time my thoughts rose like a bubble in tar. A stabbing throb strobed in my temples as rough beige walls met my bleary gaze.

Cool glass pressed to my bare skin. A diagnostic podium at my feet took readings that flittered in reverse Swahili above its sloping faceplate. Right. The village clinic. How did I get here?

As my vision cleared, a shaven-headed boy regarded me with intense eyes. He was lean and athletic like a sprinter. He seemed to have traded in his usual tie-dye tee for a bland off-white pullover that hung from only one shoulder. What was worse was the worry creasing his narrow features. Aii, what have I been putting him through? "Jambo, Youssou," I croaked.

"How are you feeling, Kukuwazuka?" he asked. Ahhh, that was his pet name for me; it means butterfly.

"Queasy."

Youssou slipped a padd from his schoolbag. "I brought your class work. There's a history exam in two days on the

Great Flood after the polar meltdowns, plus a science lesson about the Jupiter colonies. I know you're interested in such…"

"Youssou, what's wrong? How much school have I missed?"

Youssou gulped, then stuffed the padd back in his bag. "You've been in a coma for three days. While you've been sleeping, the jackals have gathered from the dunghills."

Shit…! He only fell back on metaphors when something terrible had happened. "Kalila Maji…!"

"…Hasn't been seen in three days." Youssou fetched my clothes from a cabinet adjacent to the curved archway that led into the clinic's center walkway. "Her brothers carried her home screaming, but in good health. I found you at Mokoyo Springs with your head bashed open."

"I have to see Baba." I started to rise. Not a good idea. The world spooled around my ankles. Chills rushed up my spine and set my teeth a-rattle. Youssou held my arm to steady me while simultaneously trying to gaze away from my nakedness. Once the vertigo passed, I promised that I was fine and he was free to leave so I could dress, which he did. Three days? No wonder I was famished.

"Kukuwazuka, wait. Now may not be the best time."

"Tell me more after we see Baba."

Wise Baba stalked the clinic's sitting room. He came for me, as he always had. I never noticed the fire in his eyes. Until he smacked me.

The room rushed past. Luckily a trio of stools broke my fall, and very nearly some ribs to boot. My cheek stung, but that hurt paled beside the one twisting in my heart. The slap registered in slow degrees, in time with a disbelief that I couldn't quite get around.

While I struggled to rise, Youssou struggled to hold him back. "Baba," I croaked, "why did you do that?"

Baba's bloodshot eyes narrowed as his mouth scowled. "You've dishonored us!" he shouted. "Molefe's sons say you tried to drown their sister and flay them alive."

"They're holding a kiama in three days," Youssou panted. "Mzee Molefe is bringing a daktari from Somaliland to assist him."

A kiama... a Council of Elders? "And you believed them? Baba, you should know better than that. The truth is I saved..."

Baba's hand streaked for my face again. I smacked it aside in mid-flight. His eyes and mouth frowned together, apparently not expecting this resistance. "You're mistaken, Baba," I said. "And I'm going to prove it."

I spun on my heel and left the clinic, fighting the tears damming behind my eyes. I didn't even wait for the nurses to discharge me. Sunlight blinded me, that's all. Baba couldn't have hated me. Worry compounded with pressure from the Elders must have compelled him to lash out. Yes, yes, that was a good rationalization.

The quickest route to the Molefes would be through the market. The clamor of bartering assailed us the moment we stepped into the street. Praise Ngai that Youssou was there. "Where are we going?" he asked.

"To find Kalila Maji," I said. "She knows what happened and she wasn't afraid of me. If I can talk to her, we can plead with the Elders. We won't have to bother with a kiama."

The market narrowed between stalls of breadfruit, yams, mangos, groundnuts and other produce. Cinnamon, mint and sharper spices lent their enticements to the tepid air. Hawkers of palm-sized music boxes vied with competitors across the path selling hand-crafted woodwinds and drums.

Our village is a mass of contradictions. The minarets of our small mosque compete with the brick-red dome of the Communal Hall. Market transactions are tabulated vocally on thumbnail chips. Even the footpaths, composite materials all, shine with a jade-like luster.

In part this is because we followed the admonition of the 22nd Century prophetess, Sister Jamaica. Our cities are no ostentatious affairs, say the Elders, yet their cleanliness is the envy of the Earth.

No latticed blockhouses pepper our land in the manner of the American Union. Our 'bots, too, are more streamlined, unlike the hulks that Euros lord over. Our machines blend into our gardens; theirs are blight upon it. This is true in all aspects but one.

"We may have a problem." Youssou indicated the pale, muscle-bound giantess on the Molefe's doormat. A Poppy Girl.

That name is derived from how these abominations are created. From a seed of gen-encoded protoplasm, specialists are able to grow a fully functional humanoid in a little under seven weeks. Their chief failing is that they have no brains whatsoever. One can well imagine the uses a divorcee such as Odu Molefe had for this specimen. Even I had to look up to it.

"I want to see Kalila Maji," I told it.

The Poppy Girl smiled as broadly and stupidly as a chimpanzee. "No one is allowed to see her. She is not well. Come again."

If I were fit, I'd have stormed past. But I wasn't, nor was I positive that I could rely on my power to assist me. "I'm a friend. I've not seen Kalila for several days. How is she feeling?"

It responded in a voice sweet as honeycomb. "She is doing splendidly and has made a complete recovery."

As I said, no brains. The beautiful creature cocked its head, as if suddenly aware of the contradiction in its statements. No, it looked more closely at me. "You are Jamai Dlamini. You are forbidden entry. If you persist, my instructions are to kill you."

I stepped closer instead. "You're not real. I don't have to hold back with you. Do you know who it is you're dealing with?"

"Nevertheless, you are forbidden entry. Do you wish to leave a message?"

"Yes. Tell that son of a race of dogs to prepare himself for a whipping."

Sarcasm was lost on this creature, but it felt good saying that. It acknowledged the message and resumed its vigil.

I'VE NEVER LIKED POPPY GIRLS. They are too perfect, too... perky. They always answer you with a smile and blindly do whatever menial task is required of them. They are the closest thing to slaves we have in these enlightened times.

Because they are artificial creations, there are certain prohibitions applied to their use in "demeaning situations". Their services can only be contracted under the strictest regional guidelines from the East African Community's Ministry of Science. Even then, their services can be limited to governmental security or as middle school gymnastics instructors. I wonder what Sister Jamaica would think of them. Probably she'd fight for their freedom. Yes, I think she'd...

Who was Sister Jamaica? Do they teach nothing useful in schools these days? Well, she was a pastor for an obscure parsonage in Kampala. Whether she intended it or not, certain incendiary remarks had catapulted her to celebrity status. She had observed the desperate clinging to tradition of our forebears, survivors of the final genocidal wars.

She'd suggested that tradition may be the foundation of our society, but we should not be tied blindly to a mythical golden past. The only path, she said, was forward. Not backward. Worse still, she'd had the courage to say that we must adopt technology to our needs, but it must not be viewed as some type of savior, as American futurists had claimed. Technology was a tool and must be treated as such, she said. We mustn't ever become enslaved by it.

Well, the authorities of the time weren't comfortable with such candor. First Sister Jamaica was imprisoned on a floating brig in the Sudan, some place called Abyei-Bentiu. That act served to solidify and even to expand her audience. Like all sages, she was martyred for her beliefs by another in a long line of small-minded men. But the changes she'd instituted had already taken root.

"Is that what you told him? I should like to have heard that."

"Unfortunately, he wasn't there to reap the praise," I told my daktari, S'manga Nlebela. Youssou had dragged me back to the clinic at once, where Nlebela offered disparaging remarks about my lack of judgment. This, while he waved a medicomp sprouting spider-like probes over my torso.

"Your hormone levels are elevated," he commented. "It has acted as an antidiarrhetic to enable your body to recover more swiftly."

"That's good, isn't it?"

"No! Haven't I explained the risks this protein entails? The salmonella you carry are multiplying, undoubtedly the cause of your gastrointestinal distress. You haven't sufficient immuno-reserves to compensate. Of course, if you didn't cavort with snakes, you wouldn't be harboring these bacteria!"

That was one cost of having such power. Every time it was used, it dissolved mass quantities of electrolytes from my cells. S'manga found this to be the cause of the frequent dizzy spells I experienced as a child and why I needed to take a medicinal supplement to replenish the loss.

Grandfather Esaias had his doubts about the necessity of this medicine. The notion of introducing unnatural substances into a perfectly healthy body was one that he found repellent. Still, it wasn't doing any harm. Besides, I trusted S'manga. He always kept my confidences.

"I prescribe rest," he said, "three days at the very least. Also, increase intake of your supplement by one liter daily until these bacterial levels are lowered."

"But if there is to be a kiama…"

"That will wait. I'll see to it."

Youssou's eyes flicked between us. "Is there something you're not saying? What hormone?"

I patted his hand with a smile. "There are secrets even you don't know, dear Rafiki." Drawing in a sigh, I shifted on the cot towards S'manga. "Mondo-mogo, may I ask a favor?"

"Only if you'll stop calling me that."

"Please speak for me at the kiama. More than anyone, you understand the dynamics of my power. I would appreciate it."

S'manga thumped his chest with mock severity before discharging me. I took three days rest, but I wasn't idle. There was schoolwork to catch up on and a minor bout of the trots to cope with. I also had a hearing to prepare for.

Our legal procedures are not as complicated as those of Western justice systems. Hearings are presided over by a Council of Elders. Each litigant states their case and may call whomever they choose to testify on their behalf. Once the kiama renders its decision, both sides must abide by the outcome.

It wouldn't be easy in any case. Odu Molefe served as Baba Elgonyi's Chief Steward of Public Records. Whenever any vital statistic needed to be recorded, be it matters of birth, death, or marriage, he was the man to see. In point of fact, he was in a position to see all, know all, about any individual he chose to abuse.

Indeed he was a proud man, from a proud family, and perhaps he had good reason. His clan descended from the last living members of the Acholi, a people uprooted from their farmlands by the dogs of Kony. Mzee Molefe has never forgiven the global community for ignoring the dismemberment of his ancestral culture and for turning a vital people into a band of wanderers. It was to provide roots for their children that Odu's ancestors agreed to the cooperative power-sharing plan first proposed by our father, Benjamin Dlamini, twenty generations past.

On this occasion Youssou's parents, Lazaro and Wanjiro Hadebe, provided a cot for me in their home, owing to Baba's aberrant behavior. Over breakfast the following morning they presented me with affidavits, notarized and registered in a proper legal padd. They're the dearest family in all Baba Elgonyi, and they offered more help than I ever expected.

Now, for witnesses? S'manga had already agreed to speak on my behalf. Grandmother Cele wasn't feeling well; it wouldn't be fair to expose her to the stress of this hearing. Besides, she hadn't been there. Kalila could talk, but her father had put her out of bounds.

The only other person I could call on lived in Old Nairobi. To this end Mzee Hadebe lent me access to his workstation. I hugged him six times before Youssou could peel me off him and lead me down a ramp to his home's sublevel.

Mzee Hadebe's workspace had the appearance of a vast cavern textured with cinnamon-colored rocks. Gurgling aquariums framed the station, casting an aquamarine glow over the screens. It seemed a queer arrangement, but Youssou assured me that it helped his father relax.

We must have been shuttled a dozen times between office sites before we finally accessed the East African Community's Ministry of Child Protection. I was ready to tear my hair out by the time we'd been shunted to the office of Nyassa Molefe.

"Bug," she cried as her image filled the screen. "How are you faring?"

"I've shed many skins, Nyassa," I replied. "Each has been harder to bear than the last."

Under Yousou's gentle prodding I gave Nyassa a short account of recent events. When I'd finished, she growled, "That syncopated son of a bitch."

Youssou and I blinked. We'd never heard such an expression. For my part, I couldn't see what the offspring of a menstruating dog had to do with anything.

When I asked if she would come, Nyassa snorted, "Oh I'll be there! I wouldn't miss this for all the gold of the Ashanti! By the way, do you still play with snakes? No, say nothing, it shows in your eyes. Never fear, Bug."

"Asante, Nyassa."

Over the following two days, Mzee Hadebe coached me in all the things I should say and how I should behave before the Council. When the stars rose that final evening, Youssou and I sat in the Hadebe's loft gazing through an open skylight. Lizards skritched along the walls as Youssou's warm arms enfolded me.

I'd known Youssou since we were both tots. Though he'd gained little from our friendship besides other people's scorn, he was stubborn and loyal even in the face of ridicule. And bright, too. He'll graduate a year early from Public School and plans to advance to university by fall, after his coming initiation. I'd never known a man, but should things come to that, my first choice would be Youssou.

My cheek rested on his shoulder. "Your family has been so good to me. What would happen if you ever abandoned me? What if you find another girl?"

"Oi you, look at me." Youssou took my face in his strong hands. He gazed into my eyes with an intensity that raised a shiver along my spine. "I've seen the peace that surrounds you, even if you can't seem to take part in it. I've seen the grass bend to let you pass. Remember the Long Rains? You were in the field meditating when that impala licked your nose. When you started, it should have bolted, but it didn't. It mooned over you with those sad cow eyes. If Ngai's dancers can hold you in such regard, why can't I?"

Goose pimples rose all over my skin. "Asante sana, Rafiki. I'm sorry to have taken so much time from your school proposals."

"Well, you left it a little late for that," he grinned. "I've pretty well narrowed it down to Old Nairobi University."

"May Ngai grant you success."

The Hadebes retired to bed an hour after sunset. So did I. Unfortunately, my muscles twitched like a drumhead. In time an itchy restlessness seized hold of me. I flung the covers off and wriggled into my clothes. I'd gone as far as the den when a tangle of limbs flailed beneath a blanket on the sofa. Youssou's shaven head popped up. He divined my purpose at once and whispered, "Jamai! What are you doing?"

Whoops. I thought he'd go to sleep in his own bed, not stand watch. "I… I can't sleep…"

"The hearing is tomorrow morning! You don't have time for that! Are you even well enough to..."

I shushed him with a finger to his lips. "I'll be back before dawn. I always am. Sleep well, Rafiki." I skipped from the house to the grasses beyond our village.

Near the riverbank, I found what I was looking for. A massive tube of scales basking on sun-warmed stones. She greeted my arrival with a huff, extenuating into an exploratory "ssss" as she unwound herself. A head big enough to swallow me whole rose on a silky-smooth trunk that settled around my waist.

Drawing her head to my cheek, I nuzzled the great mother in my arms. Tears ran freely now that I could unburden myself. Now that I was truly safe.

"Mama," I sniffled, "I have to talk to you. I can't believe he hit me. How could he believe I'd do such a thing? I... I thought he'd be proud."

We spoke of many things, Nyoka and I. At least, I did. We'd moved into deeper bush where she could take me fully into her embrace. A heap of coils piled behind my shoulders while her trunk expanded and contracted in easy exhalations. I'd never had an aunt to serve as a maternal figure, but Nyoka was an adequate substitute.

Ours was a different relationship than the one I had with butterflies. That totem most often acted as a spiritual balm on the many afternoons I spent alone after school, or while Baba was off on the project. When my mind is in a muddle, the butterflies come to sooth my spirit. Then the tumblers fall into place, and the answers I seek come, as they did when I was in the Temple.

Nyoka was a more imposing presence. She's never communicated to me verbally, spirit to spirit, as the butterfly has. That was beside the point anyhow. I don't go to her for wisdom; I go because I know I have her protection.

It also helped that this was a specimen from a restored species. That would certainly account for her docility. You can tell. Tip her chin and you can see the crossed flags' emblem of the New South African Federation. The entire python race was repopulated from protein sequences collected in genetic storehouses, seeded across the continent ages ago. New behavior patterns were imprinted during their restoration, to make them less dangerous to people.

"Do you know why I like you, Mama? You listen. Most people won't do that, except for Youssou. Sometimes even he doesn't understand. If not for Youssou, I'd have lost my mind many rains ago." Holding Nyoka's great neck in both hands, her tongue flicking my nose, one might wonder whether I already had.

We first came together over possession of a goat. I suppose Baba intended to teach me responsibility with this gift. No matter how many wallows I dragged that goat from, it never learned. There finally came one morning when it blundered into trouble where I almost couldn't save it. After a daylong search, I found it struggling under what I supposed to be a tree. Then I realized that it was gripped by the mother of all pythons.

Now that goat had been entrusted to me by my father and, to my six-year-old mind, Baba was Ngai. Losing that goat would have been an unforgivable offense. I grabbed a thick branch in both hands and swatted that snake's hide.

Her head swiveled around. The goat bleated and kicked free. It vanished into the thicket, leaving me, at a mere 51 kilos, to face 200 kilos of python alone. Such is gratitude.

Oddly enough, it made no attempt to defend itself. I observed deep scratches in the snake's glossy hide. Beneath her lay a mass of crushed eggs. Dog tracks and feces peppered the soil around her nest. I thought of my mother, dead so many rains, and started to cry. Here was a mother who'd lost her entire clutch. It wasn't hard to decide what to do.

I waded into a stream and waded out with a fish as big as myself. Nyoka's tongue flicked over the wriggling fish that I had to carry in both arms. "*Tafadhali, Nyoka,*" I said. "Please, take it."

Her musky odor buried itself in my nostrils. Then her head ducked behind me. There were two facts about snakes I didn't know then. First, snakes big and small swallow their prey headfirst. Second, until that moment I hadn't realized that the fish's head was pointed to my rear.

Once she had that fish in her teeth she practically jerked it from my arms. A huge coil rolled round my back, pushing beneath my skinny arms and across my belly. My tiny fists beat on its trunk, but they might as well have tried to move Kilimanjaro. Ripples flowed beneath its supple hide with each fresh gulp of fish.

Rustles behind me. First the crackle of dry grass, then soft crunches. Twisting about, I glimpsed Nyoka's tail scraping her shattered eggs from her nest. She passed me along her coils until she had laid me down in their place.

Luckily I'd settled in an upright position or her sheer weight would have squashed me. Panic would have been acceptable in this situation, but I wasn't afraid. As long as Nyoka swelled around me, I felt safe, like nothing on Earth or the stars could harm me. That night I slept with my arms encircling my serpent mother's neck.

I've learned much from Nyoka. She taught me to move swiftly and lightly, to breathe so soft even a gazelle wouldn't notice. I've also learned to listen, to distinguish in the rustle of grass between a passing locust or an approaching Elder. Yet I couldn't sleep, even here. If we could only get this stupid kiama done with. If only I could forget…

For all I'd learned about Elias, his disciple Sydelle continued to elude me. LeBeau's 26th edition of *Post Atomic Age Fringe Sects* defines the Ancient Order of Elias as a society of psychics, each person possessing a particular gift. Elias had gathered them in Old California for protection from the mob violence so prevalent in that age. Of Sydelle, LeBeau said little other than that she'd been a disciple turned to evil, that it had taken seven psychics including Elias himself to contain her. There had to be more.

I tapped the ruby linkup implanted on the back of my right hand. "Nyoka, I want to show you something." Sydelle's emblem — a woman spreading supplicating arms to the sky, piercing the darkness.

Nyoka's head periscoped on a meter of trunk, her pink tongue flicking at the neon image. Then she twisted in the opposite direction, tongue flicking faster.

Amid the song of cicadas and flies, a subtler sound arose, a moist crunch of young saplings beneath a ponderous weight. Pushing onto my knees, I grunted for Nyoka to slide off me. Then a tree smashed into my eyes.

A mask of pain pulsed around my eye sockets. How long had I been… blood welled from a searing scratch in my neck… a raspy tongue lapped this up.

My heart trembled like a Bayaka pounding a manic drumbeat. A prickly-haired monolith crushed into my stomach, probably the source of that stinging tear. My legs were bent beneath me, knees scraping a rough dirt wall. A darkness I'd never known enveloped us. I craned my neck around and bumped into a musty roof.

A voice whispered, "No one knew a daughter of Elias thrived on these faraway plains until you made inquiries into my masters."

Breath wheezed up my windpipe like shards of glass. "N… Nyoka…"

"Your companion awaits us above."

Above? How far down…? "Stuffy…can't see…"

"It is. This will facilitate our vision. It is the only place they cannot reach us, and you have no power."

"*Jina lako nani? Tafadhali,* who are you?"

"Your ancestors knew us as Ngojama." Its voice seemed ageless yet weary, like thunder after a storm. "Heed our words. There will be a man holding a crystal matrix. It feeds on the thoughts of the unwary. I know. They bound us with a portion of our own spirit and branded us with their mark. You must beware."

A huge paw guided my hand, childlike in his, to an encrustation in his oily shoulder. I jerked my hand free and tried to shove his ponderous bulk off me. I was six years old again, a mote straining helplessly against an immovable force. Ngai, please, this isn't happening! Stale breath sandpapered my lungs, throat. Can't twist free… not… fair…

Interview with Jamai Dlamini: Part 2

I WAS TIRED OF GETTING DUNKED IN THE SUDD. This time the stench was so overpowering I thought I'd puke. When Elias' pirogue sloshed through the rot, I slipped over its bow without hesitation.

Now that I was there, I felt… small, overwhelmed by his spirit. Like a skittish gazelle, I asked, "Are you truly…?"

His genial smile was answer in itself. "I'd be grateful if you'd call me friend," he said. *Ndiyo, bila shaka,* surely this was an American; why, he had no accent whatsoever.

"Asante, daktari, I'd like that." The mists rising over our keel thickened. "Where are you taking us?"

"Beats me. I'm following your lead."

We poled on to the accompaniment of a mosquito chorus. "I suppose if I'd given Sydelle more time, none of this would have happened," he said abruptly. "There was so much to do. Ultramoralists attacking anything… or person… that didn't fit their narrow view of purity."

An aged hand squeezed my shoulder. "Gifted ones such as yourself, I try to protect."

"Sydelle was my greatest failure," Elias continued. "She was untutored, afraid of what she could do. If she hadn't found that *Book of Shadows*… I shouldn't have kept it, but I'd been collecting old lore indiscriminately.

"She wanted a teacher. Instead she opened a door to what I thought was a netherworld, populated by spirits who had never known physical form. I hadn't realized then that I was only half right. What I saw was a dead sphere, a microcosm parallel to our own dimension. They'd had physical form once, but lost it."

Elias gazed across the marsh. "You're at a vulnerable time, child, like Sydelle… before she was overshadowed. For the psychically gifted, the trials of adolescence are exacerbated… damn, we're stopping."

The woman of my dreams appeared, chuckling like a silly schoolgirl. A slim figure struggled to escape her grasp. Beyond them we glimpsed other shades, similarly struggling.

"I can go no farther," Elias whispered. "Remember what I'm about to tell you. That creature," he gestured to the woman in the shadows, "taps into the well of each person's experiences. Sight, sound, even tactile senses can be magnified to make what's unreal seem real. God be with you."

"*Inshallah, daktari,*" I nodded. Before I debarked, his spirit tugged my shoulder and whispered a name, a familiar one actually. "This one would tell you more than you need to know," he said. I thanked Elias, then vaulted over the side of the pirogue.

White yungiyungi petals closed around my hips. I hadn't noticed that extra pair of arms extruding below the swell of Sydelle's breasts. These joined the first pair grasping the neck and shoulders of Kalila Maji.

Sydelle freed one hand to beckon me. Instead of four fingers, she had two, plus an oversized thumb. In the space between each knuckle sat a moist eye, round as my big toenail.

A flood of butterflies alighted on my bare skin. Even the touch of their tiny feet offered no comfort. Sydelle's olive skin glistened in the moon's pale light, illuminating full lips, a delicate nose, and lustrous raven hair.

But she had only one eye. When she bent to kiss Kalila's cheek, another eye blinked from the tresses in the back of her head. "Sydelle," I said.

Again she chuckled. "Who is Sydelle?"

"Whoever you are, then. Give me the spirit of Kalila Maji."

"Why should I?"

"Because I asked nicely, this time. Don't make me ask again."

Her eyes rolled. "Until this moment, I wouldn't have believed you were one of Elias' bitches." Her gaze fixed on the pirogue fading into mist. "He trapped us. Did he tell you that? Bound us to the mortal shell of his brat Sydelle and sealed us in amber." Then she screamed into the fog: "I was meant to bring us through!" But by then she was only shouting over empty mist. And at me.

"I… I've heard. That doesn't mean you can drag Kalila Maji out of bed anytime you like."

The fingers of her lower arm flashed like talons, slapping across my left arm. "Everything you know is a lie. Our sphere was dying, every atom literally collapsing in on themselves. We achieved total consciousness, but oh this was no enlightened choice. The darkness was closing; we had to abandon our physical shells."

Her grip tightened on my arm, twisting, pulling me closer. "We calculated that we had time enough left before the last magnetic reversal on our home, one last chance to escape the dark."

I yanked my arm away, flexing it to get back the feeling. Even in this spiritual state, her touch was like cold iron. "How can she be here?" I demanded. "Ngojama had to smother me to get me to this point."

"Ask her father. He's the idiot who's kept her sedated these past few nights."

She was still making no moves to release Kalila; indeed, she seemed to take great pleasure in nuzzling her captive's cheek. For her part, Kalila couldn't stop flailing her hands, while her mouth croaked "*niache, niache.*"

"Do either of you know what kind of power you're tempting?" Sydelle cooed in Kalila's ear.

"Do you?" I challenged.

Sydelle ran a sausage-like finger along Kalila's cheek, tracing a line to her lower lip. Then she freed one hand to flick my nose. "I'm going to enjoy consuming you." Hefting Kalila in a quadruple-forearm grip, she placed her in my arms. "Go away, little girl. I have a new playmate now."

I turned away at once. Despite allowing Kalila leave to go, that crack about "consuming me" did queer things to my stomach. I had no intention of waiting for those pasty fingers to pull me back into her nightmare. Kalila flung her arms about my neck in a python grip. Bluish fog descended over a thicket of lichen-draped vines. We moved over a bottom suddenly hard and sticky to our feet. Only the slosh of swamp water sounded in our ears. "Come here often, do you?" I asked with false cheer.

Kalila seemed to have missed that. "Every night since you rescued me, my father has sedated me," she gasped, "and every night, she brought me here. Sometimes my father comes as well, sitting on a stool reading census records while she fondles me."

"Shh," I said, "I believe your fondling days are done."

A space opened in the yungiyungi pads. The bottom appeared crystal clear, a bed of amber. Encased within was a bug, huge as a hyena, pawing with hairy forelegs at the goo. Chestnut wings like sails…

"Oh Father Ngai," I gasped. Kalila spied the image too and screamed into my shoulder.

"Why do you tremble, Lepidopteran? This is you."

Amid the overhanging lichen, Sydelle twirled, both left arms spread in an arc. "Your mind is a quagmire, girl. Desperate, confused, hemmed in by accusers. And for every question answered, a thousand new complications arise."

"My mind?" Elias' words resurfaced. If Sydelle had tapped into my subconscious, I must have the power to shape the direction this vision took. "Sister, do you trust me?"

Said Kalila, "Yes! Yes!"

"Good, because we're going home." My thoughts focused on a dwelling blazoned with rich tapestries and Odu Molefe reclining in a bamboo seat near the door. A surge of annoyance spurred me to spring.

My feet padded over a cool jade footpath. The fog dissipated before Kalila Maji's home. Odu Molefe sat just as I'd imagined. Or was it mere imagination? A sudden impulse seized me, and so I flicked his oversized ear.

Flailing limbs preceded a nasty fall. Molefe jumped from his tumbled chair and stared about wildly. Neither of us gave ourselves away as we giggled. Then I snuck inside.

A pride of lion cubs covered the quilt that padded Kalila's sleep mat. Her body breathed in intermittent sighs. She seemed to gaze down at it as though this couldn't quite be herself. I lowered Kalila's spirit onto her slumbering form. This filmed over her physical body, which shuddered before relaxing.

One of us was safe. As my own spirit glided through her wall, a precipice yawned before me. Wind rushed past, my limbs flailed, and Mokoyo Springs gushed into my nostrils.

A silky smooth leg jammed between my thighs. Lips pressed to mine. It happened quickly. One moment they were there, soft and inviting; the next, Sydelle tossed a pair of arms around me. "Well done, brat. It wasn't very helpful though, was it?"

She had a point. I'd freed Kalila, but I was still trapped in Sydelle's clammy embrace. I tried to push her away, but her other pair of hands crept spider-like behind my back.

"Why do you resist?" she crooned. "We both know the pains of loneliness. Poor girl, you're right, we have many experiences to draw on. Every life we touch becomes part of our collective consciousness. But yours are so much more vivid."

"Please, why here? This place is sacred."

"Only to you. It's your safe place, the memory that's strongest in your young mind."

Her dual-fingered paws brushed through the thick of my hair until they joined at the scalp. The other pair massaged the roundness of my breasts in slow, even strokes. A drum seemed to pound inside my chest as my phantom limbs trembled. I'd kill Ngojama for putting me through this. "W... what are you doing?"

"Giving you what you desire. Feeding on the burning hunger within the two of us."

"Is... is that Sydelle talking, or the shade who possesses her?"

She answered with a smile reflected in hungry eyes. "You came to learn of me? Come, see."

She inclined her head, and I followed the direction of her gaze. We were still in Mokoyo Springs. But the Moon was gone. A massive orb filled its space, filled nearly the entire sky, but for one narrow sliver near its upper hemisphere. Clouds of the purest blue blanketed its surface, if it had any, clouds layered with chalk-white jet streams. Occasionally its troposphere was punctuated with crackles of lightning, traversing an entire hemisphere. "Is that...?"

"No," Sydelle replied with an eye as full of wonder as mine. "Our home was in orbit around what you see, our Parent Body. The core of our home was a powerful magnetic orb with predictable magnetic reversals that acted in conjunction with those of our Parent Body's poles. On those dates, we could see into other realms as the barriers separating each sphere thinned due to the two bodies' electromagnetic reverses.

"Some spheres were infinitesimal, some agreeable enough to support a meager system of life. Some were vast, like yours, with stars numbering like grains of sand. But our escape had an element of chance. We didn't know what was the condition of the sphere we fled to. We had no choice but flight. That haste was our undoing.

"We slipped through the barrier surrounding our home, as easily as a pebble slips through a soap bubble. We arrived in a place of frigid darkness. That sphere had achieved a state of total entropy even before our time began. Without access to the magnetic reversals of our home and our Parent Bodies, we were trapped.

"Now can you still talk to me of loneliness?"

I should not have let her get me so engrossed. While the purple sky shimmered above, below arms were flowing about my hips. A flush rose in my belly as Sydelle thrust her face in the water and buried herself in my bosom. Soft lips began to suck at my nipples. "Open yourself to me," she whispered. "Grant me passage."

With every tender kiss my breath came in shorter and shorter pants. For one insane moment I felt whole. Devil take the kiama, this threatened to rock me to my heels. I'd waited so very long for Youssou to…

What was I doing? She was trying to distract me, burrow into my…

Sydelle's sultry tones brushed through my thoughts. "You can't fight this. You don't want to. You want to be touched like this, just one time."

Yes, yes. But I wanted it from Youssou. Every time I closed my eyes I saw his face. Every salt-damp breath reminded me of his scent. Those sensations of him grounded my next train of thought. My mind filled with the experience that had got me into this stupid mess.

A loud crack jarred the air. Two massive trunks whooshed from above. The first plunged into Sydelle's chest, wrenching us apart. The second, a scaly trunk smacked into my cheek. A massive comforting coil engulfed my waist, hoisting me toward the tree's highest branches.

A copper-skinned arm stretched from the canopy above. Not Elias. This face, somehow familiar, grinned from the white-flowered branches. Cinnamon curls cascaded around oval features. Her eyes appeared wise, mirthful.

"Well placed," she said. "Elias sends his greetings. Come to me, child."

I hung suspended in a serpent's coil, gazing at the proffered hand, wanting to believe, but afraid it was only a vision-induced fantasy. "Are you…?"

Steam blew around my ankles. The stench of blood rose on the mists. Talons lunged from the springs on impossibly elastic limbs. "Give me your hand!" the woman cried.

I needed little persuasion. Both my hands clasped her wrist. She yanked me into the leafy canopy as an anguished shriek soared from below.

When I opened my eyes, I was back beside the stream.

And so I greeted the dawn of a new day, naked as a baby chimpanzee. The predawn light cast the snowcaps of the Aberdere Mountains in pink highlights. The nippy chill did nothing to ease my cramped muscles. So much for a restful night.

I brushed rust-tinted soil from my skin. Glancing toward home, I spied what appeared to be a very stout tree. Or so I believed until it breathed. My hand started to my mouth, then fell to my lap. "Ngojama, I presume?"

"The same," he rasped. In terms of sheer muscle, he seemed more ape than man. Spots peppered his oily hide. Additionally, a high crest of bristles stemmed from the crown of his head to his mid-back.

"Now do you understand the enemy we face?" he rumbled. "They require your vessel, your body, to use as a conduit for the inhabitants of the Other World, as had their Mistress Sydelle before Elias incarcerated her… What?"

That last was on account of the dirt clod I'd pitched into the back of his neck. "Couldn't you have just told me that, you over-anxious turd of a baboon?"

"You flatter yourself, insect. Had you heeded us while you were comatose several days ago, this would not have been necessary. We cannot be aided in ignorance."

Tiny feet alighted on my bosom. Butterfly wings spread to shield my nakedness. Where one is unable to abide by one's own modesty, the spirits provide. "That was you? You projected those images into my head? Who the bloody hell do you think you are?"

Ngojama's barbed tail swished like a wild dog's as it sniffs prey. "We are the Hidden, born of fire before the days of the prophets who drove us to the Wastes. We roamed the forests near the Tana River. When your ancestors dwindled in unbelief, when science became your religion, our species withered and died. All but I."

"A considerably vague parable," I sighed. "Well, there is one other thing you can do, oh massive one."

He inclined his head as I spoke of trials and Poppy Girls. He warned me again of the man with the crystal matrix. Then the ground rumbled beneath my buttocks. In a flash Ngojama burrowed into the earth. When I staggered to my feet a more immediate problem arose.

Where were my clothes?

I'd left them on a branch last night. They should be right in front of me. May fleas devour his eyes. I couldn't prance back to Baba Elgonyi like this, not at daybreak. Tapping an auto-recall code into my wrist-linkup, I cried, "Youssou, my clothes are gone. Help me, please."

"I knew those snakes would get you in trouble someday, Bug."

I gulped. "Nyassa?"

"Keep out of sight, we'll home in on your frequency."

"Asante…wait!" A new thought struck me. "Nyassa, would you ask Youssou to stop at my home? There's a parcel in green tissue under my cot, and I want it."

"Is my father going to like this?"

"I sincerely doubt it."

One could almost hear the smile in Nyassa's reply. "You'll have it, Bug. Stay tight, we're on our way."

When I stepped from the bush to greet Youssou, Nyassa, and Mama Hadebe, Nyassa dropped the parcel. This baffled me until I looked down at her. Before her father sent Nyassa away nine rains past, I stood at her bosom. Today she was about eye-level with my chin. "I don't know if I should call you Bug anymore," she whistled.

The first thing Mama Hadebe noticed, however, upon opening the parcel was the embroidery on the back of my new homemade waistcoat. "Child! You're not going to wear this to the kiama?" she exclaimed.

"I most certainly am."

"Well. This will cause quite a row."

And that was the end of it. The outfit wasn't nearly complete, but it would do. Mama Hadebe lent me a ruffled blouse to wear under the blue waistcoat, plus a short turquoise skirt. My feet remained bare, which suited me fine. I grinned at Youssou's slack-jawed, salivating stare. Finally I said, "Shall we go?"

The basso of drums laid a counterpoint to the morning song of bee and bird. There are events in my life I can recall with absolute clarity. I've forgotten every exam I'd taken in school, yet I can visualize every detail of our class trip to the Masai Mara ten rains ago. Being dunged by my fellow age grade students helped in that regard.

So it was today. Nyassa parked her bat-winged skiff thirty meters from the old baobab that predated our village. I'd requested the kiama convene here, rather than in the Communal Hall they preferred. Clouds misted around distant cobalt hills. Trees formed a green belt that receded to the horizon.

Youssou lifted me from the skiff's rear seat. Drummers flanked the nine Elders sitting cross-legged around the bole of the sacred tree, each man in his choice of casual wear. They needn't have feared for their comfort either. Their temporary awning re-circulated cool air, pumped through the bellies of the squat *mahuti* service 'bots book-ending them. The drummers' hands slowed in mid-beat once we came into view, then stopped altogether.

Mama was right; my outfit caused quite a stir. Doubtless it was the emblem on my back: two hands bracing seven candle flames. As we advanced, the spectators drew back. *Totos* eyed us quizzically before their heads got stuffed into their parents' armpits. The oldest men-folk actually stamped to their feet.

Oh, I liked this.

A white face emerged from among my people. His head appeared to have been chiseled from a granite block; the deep furrows lining his cheeks and chin only reinforced the impression. Most of his pepper-gray hair had receded past his brow, which allowed an amiable pair of hazel eyes to gaze back at me. A plain off-white smock and slacks comprised his garments. This would be Odu Molefe's hired daktari. Well then, bring him on.

I spotted S'manga Nlebela's blue-green smocks amid the innermost ring of spectators. He began his usual inclination, but a change came over him. Actually it was mostly in his eyebrows that furrowed so deeply I thought he might be in pain. Rising stiffly, he strode briskly through the onlookers to join our party. "What the devil happened to you?" he demanded in an undertone.

"I... I misplaced my clothes. Look, I'm not that late..."

"I mean your eyes! What did that to... wait." S'manga fumbled in a pocket of his smock and passed me a mirror. With his hands steadying mine, I tipped it so I too could study the spots of blood in both corneas. Thanks to Ngojama, I had a lovely ring of purple discoloration surrounding my eye sockets to match.

Nyassa slipped between us. She'd already set to work with her compact to try to minimize my unsightliness. "Relax, doc," she said, "She's only been playing with her snakes."

"Putting aside the poor wisdom in choosing last night for such an activity," S'manga rejoined, "why are there no new micro-fractures in her ribs? These symptoms are inconsistent with her usual nocturnal ramblings. Child, for the love of Heaven…"

"I… I don't think I could explain," I said, then trailed off at S'manga's droopy, disappointed stare.

"Child, you told me you wanted everything to come out today. This is a hell of a time to go back to withholding information, especially from us." His wave encompassed everyone in my party.

What was I supposed to say? I didn't even understand what happened last night, let alone have time to absorb and explain it to all and sundry. "It's… it's not relevant to what we came to do here, daktari," I said.

"Do you feel well enough? Really?" he pressed. I nodded, to which he hissed through his teeth, "Then I'd guess we'd best get started." And the long march resumed.

Finally we reached the canopy of branches at the center of the gathering. Odu Molefe seemed to shrink into himself. "At last you show your true colors," he said. This troubled me, but I let it pass.

An aide touched his padd. In response, a translucent screen of chartreuse letters flickered before the Elders. As butterflies settled on my bare arms, I came forward to give a statement.

"Reverend Grandfathers," I said, lowering my gaze. "There has been a terrible misunderstanding. The sons of Mzee Molefe speak half-truths colored by affection for their sister. I was at Mokoyo Springs, but that is because I always go there to swim. It is a private place.

"Kalila Maji would never have known I was there if a Nightcrawler hadn't attacked her and breached her vest. I drove the Nightcrawler off. I didn't hurt her. I would never hurt her. I petition the kiama to dismiss this hearing on that basis. Asante Sana, Grandfathers."

Molefe's expert called as I backed away. "One moment, please. Why would you help this girl, fraulein?"

"What did you expect me to do?" I demanded. "I couldn't stand by and do nothing…"

A sharp pain stabbed behind my eyeballs. Mama Hadebe and Nyassa rushed to support me until the pain subsided. "I'm all right," I whispered.

"Good," said Nyassa. "Now don't do that again. He's trying to goad you into making a bad impression. Don't let him."

"I hear, Nyassa."

"And stop being so damned formal while you're about it."

Molefe's hireling had approached the Elders. "Gentlemen," he began in a guttural but genial accent, "I am Bren Auflauring, Doctor der Philosophie and a resident at Dobra Damo Rehabilitative Services. If it pleases you, my credentials."

Daktari Bren (I say it this way because his surname is too hard to pronounce) passed over a padd that the kiama scrutinized. "I come to assess the mental competence of this fraulein. And also," he continued, "to dispel any illusions regarding her supposed magic."

Taking his cue, S'manga came forward. "No magic is involved," he said. "Jamai's abilities abide by definitive biochemical and physical processes."

"We have not met, *mein herr*," Bren said, extending a hand. It was not taken. "You are…?"

"I am the accused's primary physician. I have studied Jamai for nine rains and I can say with absolute confidence that no one here is better qualified to elucidate the truth of her abilities."

"Be aware of this, then," Molefe said, "if she is as mentally unstable as we suspect, I will petition the kiama to commit her to Dobra Damo RS for the good of Baba Elgonyi and her own well being."

Affidavits from Hwenge, Mutu, and the Hadebes were entered into the record. Psychological assessments dating back to my earliest preschool years followed. Sunlight focused like a lens on our skins, baking us to a slow crisp. Then a white-haired Elder flicked his wrist. It was time.

"Daktari," I said, "tell them what you once told me."

S'manga inclined his head to the council. "Fellow Elders, every creature metabolizes energy, often more than they require to sustain themselves. Jamai is able to tap into that reservoir of energy and redirect it through conscious effort of will to perform any task when required.

"Such an accumulation of energy would be disruptive to the flow of her neural pathways. My research has uncovered an anomaly. Jamai's cells are permeated with an unusual hormone, which shields her nervous system from the biological power she channels."

"These findings have no relevance," Bren protested.

"On the contrary," S'manga snorted, "it has absolute relevance, as our people's fear of Jamai is based on ignorance of her abilities. By removing that element we take her power out of the realm of superstition, and into the bowels of science."

"What effect have these hormones on her mental stability?"

"None. If I may use an analogy, these chemicals act as a fluid insulation enabling biological energy to be conducted through her body and thereby safely expelled. It appears to have no relation to intellectual or emotional development."

"So far as you know," Bren suggested.

"Yes," S'manga nodded grudgingly.

"You knew this," Molefe growled, "and never revealed it to the Council? Why?"

S'manga lanced Odu with a stare that marked him as an imbecile. "Have you never heard of doctor-patient confidentiality? Jamai has never requested that I divulge these facts and I have respected her silence. Moreover, she has never used her gifts to harm anyone, and I do not believe it is in her nature to do so."

S'manga bowed low to the kiama, whose members nodded in turn. He faded behind Nyassa, who stepped forward with a smile. She was as thin as her brothers, but better dressed in an elegantly creased velvet jumpsuit. "Let me at him," she said.

"From an unimpeachable witness to a questionable one," Bren smirked. "Tell me, Doctor Molefe, by what irony are you speaking on this girl's behalf?"

The throb in my temples momentarily flared. I clenched my jaws until the pain eased, but missed Nyassa's reply.

"...known you were her greatest tormentor as a child," Bren was saying. "Weren't you the one who called her *mother-killer*?"

Nyassa's lips compressed. I'll admit to a flash of bitterness, a feeling that quickly passed. "Yes," she said. "I was stupid enough to believe such crap."

"What changed?" This I wanted to hear for myself.

"You did, Bug."

Hands on hips, the old Nyassa swaggered before the gathering. "This girl had no reason to like me, but when our class went on an outing to the Masai Mara she went out of her way to cultivate a friendship with me. In return... I talked our class *totos* into dunging her. She could have run. But all she did was stand there and take it. And she still tried to be friends. I knew then the stories my father had told me were lies. It was for that reason he sent me away."

"Really?" Bren feigned disinterest, but his theatrical tone worried me. "Is it not also true," he said, advancing on Nyassa, "that this fraulein has butterflies and snakes for playmates?"

Nyassa didn't budge, even when his breath blew in her face. "Fraternization with animals isn't unusual," she replied. "North Americans have kept exotic pets for centuries. Part of that is pure intimidation, part because these creatures are more arousing than your average rheumy-eyed mutt. Documented cases exist of children raised by wolves and other wild species."

"But Mowgli... excuse me... Jamai is not a feral child," Bren countered. "Nor are all her friends' pets. She receives high marks in school and interacts well enough with others, when it suits her. And still she has animal mentors, one innocuous, the other potentially life-threatening. Do you honestly believe such associations do not warrant therapy?"

Nyassa studied me for the longest time. Then her mouth set in resolution. "Was Wangari Maathai crazy to link conservation to our social values?"

Bren's mouth opened. He fumbled for his padd, still in the hands of our prosecuting Elders. Nyassa pressed her attack. "Some of Jamai's behavior is aberrant, but that's hardly proof of insanity."

"I had not implied as such..."

"Oh no? By your own admission, she is a bright student. Plus she has an intuitive awareness of her problems, and that's a good start. If she needs help in adjusting to her social conditions, it should come from those who care about her welfare, close to home."

"You can say this… you, who haven't spoken to the fraulein for nine years?"

"It might interest you to know that my sister Kalila has been watching Jamai on my behalf since my father shipped me to Eritrea for re-education. Her letters support my assumptions."

"Doctor Molefe, I wonder… when Jamai petitioned you, did you see an opportunity to redress past wrongs?"

I zipped between him and Nyassa. "Why are you saying these things? Nyassa hasn't done anything."

"Two words, fraulein. Personal bias!"

Bren addressed the kiama. "We intend to establish a basis for hostility against the Molefe clan. That such hostility exists is evident by abuse heaped on this poor fraulein by said clan over her short lifetime."

Odu Molefe bellowed, "Whose side are you on?"

Nevertheless, Dr. Bren continued. "These factors cumulated in an assault on the helpless Kalila Maji, whose brothers' neglect placed her in a dangerous predicament. Given Jamai's manifest hatred for the…"

"I don't hate Odu Molefe."

Nobody could have been more surprised at what I said than I was. Bren's impressive jaw jutted forward. "What did you say?" he whispered.

"I don't want to hate Odu Molefe. I've never wanted to hate anyone. All I want to understand is why he's frightened of me."

"That's rubbish!" Molefe screamed.

"Doesn't sound crazy to me," Nyassa commented.

"Look at him." Taking Bren's arm, I turned him to espy Molefe. "See how he hangs back, how his eyes dart like a weaverbird's as it drinks at the well. He fears…"

Aii! A livid pulse pounded at my skull. I would've staggered if Bren hadn't caught my arm. Most kindly he whispered, "Are you all right, Lepidopteran?"

What did he call me?

My head swelled with agony, twisting every muscle inside out. A rainbow of spots shimmered before my eyes. I couldn't take this! S'manga wouldn't have let me come if I wasn't well.

Through blurring vision, I noticed Bren's hand cupped over his right hip pocket. It'd been in that position before, but it hadn't seemed important… aii! There… a rounded shape swelled against the crease of his slacks… his matrix.

"It's… you!" Ngojama had warned me. This was the man.

Butterflies clustered thickly around me, lending me their strength and intelligence. I didn't need to see this matrix he wielded to act; the shape would be enough. I trained my thoughts on his pocket, then visualized Ngai smashing Bren's ball in his teeth.

Perspiration chilled my spine as my fist tightened. From what seemed a distance, glass crinkled, before it crunched.

Bren's pupils bulged. Incense-scented smoke soon wisped from his slacks. The pain vanished, and I knew it wouldn't return. I fixed him with a glare that said: *no more tricks.*

He inclined his head, perceiving the changed circumstance. He in turn lifted a gold watch on a chain around his waist, and flicked it open. As Odu Molefe stepped beside Bren, my knees turned to water. A raised bronze symbol had been imprinted on the watch's cover-plate: a woman with raised arms, inside a broken circle. The goldsmith had been mistaken about the number of eyes she had, and where, but that was beside the point.

I knew then that Odu Molefe was only a pawn of the Children of Sydelle. He always had been. Bren was his true master. And I wasn't ready to face them.

Bren's knuckles screwed thoughtfully into his nostrils. "I've underestimated you," he said and drifted away.

Underestimated me? I didn't know what I was doing. For that matter… where was Youssou? I swerved left and right. A sea of confused and hostile faces girded me. Where had he gone? I needed him.

Did I dare tell the kiama what I knew? Sweet Ngai, what did I know? Mostly symbols and impressions, plus a vision I didn't understand. What did that prove? What if they asked about Elias? This waistcoat marked me as his disciple. I couldn't explain the nature of my training either. That would mark me as a madwoman. If I kept my mouth shut, said as little as possible…

I'd decided on this course of action as Molefe approached, keeping a respectful distance between us. Fright resonated through his guarded query. "This costume. Where did you find it?"

"I made it." There, that was true enough.

His sandals scraped unnaturally loud on the ground as he paced behind me. A finger dragged along the cloth on my back. "What an interesting emblem. Why haven't you displayed it before?"

"I… I didn't know about it until a few months ago…"

"That I find difficult to believe." I didn't blame him. I sounded unconvincing to myself.

"I don't understand."

"Are you saying you didn't know that your mother was a child of Elias?"

One of my empathic gifts is the ability to sniff out the truth when it is spoken. It's difficult to quantify. I can only describe it as an all-consuming fire inside the belly. That sensation burned strongly within me now.

"Mama…?"

Molefe advanced, and somehow I retreated. "Don't deny it!" he screamed. "You must have known! She had power like yours and she wasn't afraid to use it!"

Baba, who'd been silent and withdrawn, rose from the ranks of Elders like a thundercloud. "Speak the truth, Molefe. You feared my wife because you could hide nothing from her, therefore you've transferred your terrors onto my daughter. In regard to her power, I'd say our ancestors were exceptionally generous to her."

"Mzee, the people of Elias are not a threat," I said, drawing Molefe's attention back to me. "Why must you fear…?"

"Be silent! We know the histories. We were once divided into factions within factions within factions. For 400 rains we have been free of the stink of foreign influence. Your mother with her magic would have steered us back onto the path of ignorance and chaos. I could not allow that."

Odu swung to the kiama with pleading hands. "This bitch is another Alice Lakwena in the making. Already she claims to talk to the spirits of bugs and snakes. Is it not a small step to her leading off our young people to follow her on a path of cleansing? You know what Lakwena brought on our brothers in the north. This man…" his finger stabbed the air, to where Bren stood uncomfortably staring at his sandals "…may be the only hope to keeping her on the straight and narrow path. Let me help her!"

Baba's quiet rumble cut into Molefe's diatribe. "Why don't you tell her what you did, fisi? Tell my daughter you were the Dispatch on Duty at the Office of Emergency Services when my wife was in childbirth. Tell her you waited two hours before summoning medical aid."

No, it wasn't possible.

"I didn't know her condition was so serious," Molefe said. "I didn't think she'd die."

Interview with Jamai Dlamini: Part 3

IN A DAZE, I SHUFFLED TO BABA, oblivious of the Elders chattering among themselves, and doubtless coming to a summary judgment. "Baba, you knew?"

Then another player entered the stage. "Reverend Grandfathers, I wish to speak." Five meters beyond the outward-growing circle of faces stood Youssou, wringing a bloody fist. Beside him stood Kalila Maji.

Molefe's muscles writhed as though an apoplexy had seized him. It seemed he could only watch as his youngest offspring brushed through the murmuring crowd. Youssou hurried to my side. "How?" I began.

"It wasn't easy," Youssou whispered. "The only person who knew what had happened between you two was Kalila Maji. While everyone was focused on Nyassa, I slipped away."

"Did his Poppy Girl do this?" I touched his raw knuckles.

"I'm getting to that. Actually, that Amazon lay spread-eagle on a fresh-turned mound of earth. Hwenge was trying to drag Kalila back inside their home. He made some off-color remark about my parentage…"

"Ahh." I perceived Ngojama's sly hand in that Amazon's state of unconsciousness.

Kalila no longer seemed the mouse. Defiance shone in her eyes and spirit in her stride. Her high adolescent tones commanded the day.

"Grandfathers," she said, "what my brothers told you is a dunghill of lies. I'm surprised no one had questioned this, given their records of truancy. They left me alone at Mokoyo Springs.

While they were gone, a Nightcrawler attacked me. Jamai Dlamini saved me. She drove the Nightcrawler away, and she didn't use any power to do it. After that she carried me to shore and wrapped me in her own towel, which I still have to return.

"She made no threats, asked for no rewards and in return…" Her thumb jabbed over her shoulder toward the outskirts of Baba Elgonyi. "My brothers tried to kill her. Jamai's not crazy. She's saner than anybody in my immediate family. I come before you to demand that you deny my father's request for incarceration."

The kiama huddled together for several minutes. After a heated discussion, they beckoned Odu Molefe and me into the baobab's shadow.

On behalf of the Elders, Mzee Hadebe spoke. "We have heard many strange stories today, some only half as bizarre," he chuckled, "as the tales written of us by Euros during Colonial times. However, idiosyncratic though her lifestyle may be, Jamai Dlamini has demonstrated much courage in placing young Kalila's life above her own. Moreover, despite countless opportunities she has never used her gifts against another living spirit.

"It is the judgment of this kiama that Odu Molefe's judgment has been impaired by concern for his daughter, and that Jamai Dlamini is to be praised for her actions. With all respect to Daktari Auflauring, we do not find sufficient grounds to commit her to his facilities."

It's over. Praise Ngai, it was over. I wanted to rush to Kalila and give her a dozen hugs. Nyassa, however, was already lavishing her with hugs of her own.

People gathered up their mats and cushions and little ones. Gossip had already begun to circulate over the Elders' decision. Bren tried to brush past in the general breakup, but I caught his elbow.

"You're no daktari," I said. "And Dobra Damo is no hospital. You'd have sent me to one of your outposts. Why are you doing this?"

He eyed me blandly. An old bloated matron wriggled between us, and he slipped away. The Hadebes showered me with hugs, but I still wanted to thank Kalila for what she'd done for me. If her father had his way, I might never see her again.

That evening I raised a fish to the master of the forest. While I scuffed dirt under my heel, Ngojama spit fish bones from both sides of his mouth. I spoke of my fears, when Youssou traveled to Old Nairobi after the fall rains. Would he forget me, or find a better girl? Perhaps I should have kept quiet, but who was he going to talk to? The Mombassa Wire Service? Who else was I going to tell? That hearing had left me more isolated than ever.

Somehow, while I'd been talking to the ground, my face nestled in Ngojama's coarse-haired chest. His musk scent was strong, with a touch of fresh-turned earth. Arms like two supple trees encircled me. It's strange, but when I'm with people it's as if I'm dodging spears. It's in the embrace, which should frighten me, that I feel most comforted.

Dawn found me perched on a fallen tree overlooking the spring where this whole unpleasant episode began. On this humid morning, the egg-stench reeked much stronger. Youssou hunched beside me, hiding his nose and saying nothing. Still, having a listening ear seemed enough.

"I can't believe he didn't tell me about Mama," I said. "How could he have kept something this important a secret? I'm afraid to ask what else Baba is hiding."

There was more than mere discomfort in the silence that fell between us. Everyone knew Odu's family background. The story of every family in Baba Elgonyi was no secret to anyone.

Everyone knew Alice Lakwena and her successor, Joseph Kony, had killed the Acholi, both their culture and their lives.

Even so, I'd been so caught up in my own troubles that it never occurred to me Odu might associate me, or Mama for that matter, with Lakwena. Wearing that uniform to the kiama hadn't helped things at all.

When I think of it, the two of us aren't so different. Alice Lakwena also claimed the ability to communicate with the spirits of animals, and in fact her contention was that those very spirits spurred her to take up arms against the ruling party of the time. I had no intention of starting a war or a movement centered around my personality. But it must have appeared that way to Odu, what with my associating myself with Elias. I didn't know how to soothe his fears; I had no idea how our lives would sort out.

"May I join you?"

We both started at that timorous voice. Kalila Maji stood expectantly at the other end of the log. Youssou stroked my back, then sprang up and sauntered up the trail to Baba Elgonyi. She scurried past him to sit beside me. I tried inching further along the bark, but Kalila scooted closer until our legs touched.

"I never had a chance to thank you," I said.

"You saved me. Twice, actually. We're even. Nyassa never told me you were so shy. Or so big."

"I didn't use to be."

Conches and amber rattled as her head rested in the crook of my neck. It warmed me inside that she could trust me so much. Made me nervous, too. "Why haven't you talked to me before?"

"Father forbade it. My brothers have been very overprotective since he sent Nyassa away." Then she kissed my neck. "As long as I have you here, may I ask you a favor? Would you teach me to swim?"

"R... right now? Won't your father object?"

"Probably. What's your point?"

Muscles tugged at the corner of my mouth. A smile? I hoped so. "All right. Follow me."

We spent many an hour at Mokoyo Springs practicing strokes and, of course, floating. Jackals abounded in human guise within the walls of Baba Elgonyi. It's good to know there are some I could call friend, too.

ASIDES: A BETTER WORLD
More recollections of Jamai Dlamini

THERE WAS NO OTHER POSSIBLE END to the old oil economy than disaster. Too many industries were tied into it. When the wells were finally all tapped out, it wasn't simply those industries that went with it.

Entire nations whose livelihoods revolved around petroleum crumbled into fundamentalism and anarchy, from which only a few survived. The story of the midnight flight of the Saudi royal family to Switzerland is still related to our children, an amusement to remind them of the fate awaiting all those who aspire to royalty on the backs of others.

Concurrently, this also heralded the end of mass-market consumerism. The availability of raw materials and the ensuing collapse of trade relations between nations rendered this impractical. The manufacture of goods and services gradually had to become focused on local needs. In time, people realized you didn't need to drown yourself in impractical garbage to attain happiness. The day the dollar died indeed was one of great rejoicing.

Power... hmmm. Unfortunately, in Europe and the Americas there was a brief flirtation with alternate energy sources, nuclear being only the most obvious. For Mother Africa, our path led to a diversification of resources. Our power grid was wedded to the gifts of the Sun and Mother Earth.

Solar sails, high in the atmosphere, convert the Sun's rays into stored energy that is transmitted down kilometer-long cables tethered to generators on the ground. Geothermal taps strung along the Great Rift Valley and the Ethiopian highlands add their power to the grid, as well as what you'd call more eco-friendly hydroelectric works.

They say in times of need, the right leader will step forward. In the case of the American Union, quite the opposite was true. Their imperious leader thought he'd found the perfect solution to their perpetual immigration problem to the south. What? encourage equitable work opportunities in Mexico? Nah. Instead, they invaded the Republic of Mexico.

(Not long after they tried to do the same with their northern neighbor, Canada, and received their third drubbing in as many years at the hands of the Canadians. It's not entirely true to call it the "American" Union, as Canada solidly retains its independence.)

Oh, there is no "world government" nonsense going on. Our lands are more decentralized in the aftermath of the Lost Age; power had been taken out of the hands of any single individual. Plus, all the Big Men who'd oppressed us before were gone, one way or another. And frankly, we were tired of war, all of us.

Our Elder-ancestors set up a system of five Communities in Africa. Each Community is governed by a weak central government, further divided into smaller districts serving a handful of villages. Control remains in the people's hands. In times of crisis, our Communities form short-term alliances, quickly dissolved when the danger is past. Except, that is, in one particular case…

People still needed land, as the in-rushing seas had driven many thousands from their coastal homes. Conversely, the desert was still encroaching on our settlements, pushing us in the opposite direction. To alleviate both these concerns, a project was conceived to re-green the desert and undo the catastrophe people had wrought so many centuries earlier. The designers knew this could not be accomplished in a single generation or even multiple ones.

This project would have to be advanced over decades, centuries, if need be. On that basis, the Sahara Reclamation Project was begun, of which my father has held such a great part. His role in the Project's present generation was more relevant to more than I ever realized, and I'm afraid I'll have to leave that tale for my man Youssou to tell.

MORATHI

WHEN THE PSYCHIC SHOCK ROCKED THE MORATHI, he perceived something had gone terribly wrong. Moreover, he realized from the concurrent patterns of thought and the purity of their construction, that it had come from his granddaughter twenty generations removed.

A lightning storm approached, charging the atmosphere with ions. This he would use to his advantage. Gathering his essence, he slipped from the temple of Elias. For two heartbeats he existed as a string of electron energy bound by his will alone. In truth, he overshot his objective by four kilometers before arriving near a stand of figs.

He resumed material form, such as it was, preparing for the worst. Yes, it was she. His granddaughter's biochemical patterns were as familiar to his e-band senses as scent and sight would render her to any living mortal. Over the preceding centuries, he had also learned to determine meaning in the cycling of neural activity and irregularities in their functions.

Still, on this night these extra-human senses were hardly necessary. The foliage-print of her garments had been lost beneath a splatter of gelatinous goo. Trace minerals within the substance suggested that its source had been gen-derived humanoid tissue.

The girl stared at her hands. Just stared, trembling as though she'd explode from her own vibrations. Her mouth formed words too soft-spoken to be discerned.

"Let me take you home," he offered, extending an ethereal hand.

She seemed oblivious to this and all other things. "…didn't mean to," she whispered. "I didn't know that would happen."

A mountainous shadow weaved through distant trees, one bearing a stiff crest along its scruff. It hadn't seen her yet. "We have to leave," he insisted, taking her arm.

A small energized pulse traveled through his hands up the neuropathways in her arm. He detested this manipulation, more so since she was his own kin. He consoled himself with the knowledge that circumstance warranted such urgent action. His pulse stimulated a small sector in her brain tissue, willing her legs to move. He steadied the girl as she stood. A glint of pink caught his attention.

At a whim, the square of polyresin floated from her wrist linkup onto the tip if his finger. Her identification chip, obviously. The information would ordinarily be quite comprehensive: name, residence, medical requirements, et al. This he could easily read through his photon-sensitive senses. Or might have been, had the chip still contained any information at all.

"Wiped? Child, what's happened? What are you saying?"

Her head turned at the rise in pitch of his voice. Her jade eyes appeared so glazed he might have poured sand over them and she'd never have known the difference. With a dead sigh, she repeated the words she'd apparently been saying all along:

"Grandfather, I don't exist."

HYENA'S PROMISE

(Narrated to the author by Youssou Hissen Hadebe)

Day One: The Tenacious Bonds of Home

"Do you think she'll come?" I asked.

Father pursed his lips, as he often did when lost in thought. The retractable roof of his skiff shielded us from the sun's worst rays. We'd been waiting on the plains outside our village since early afternoon, with only the skiff's cooling system to relieve the stuffiness.

"I'm certain of it." His voice boomed naturally. "We've left small gifts near the old baobab. Bowls of dates, gourds of mango juice, extra supplies of her electrolyte medicine. The dishes are always returned to that spot clean... ahh."

Fifty meters ahead, a small figure rose from the savannah. No, not so small. Father observed my sharp exhalation and asked, "What's the matter?"

"N... nothing. I hadn't realized she'd gotten so... tall."

Father toggled a switch. The vaulted arch of the roof slid back into the rear chassis. "Go to her," Father said.

I nodded and left the skiff. The brittle grass of summer keened as I rushed to greet her. Nine months of bachelor studies at Old Nairobi University had dulled my memories of home, but I always remembered my childhood friend. When last I saw her, I could have sworn she was still a skinny runt.

A man becomes accustomed to friends remaining within the fixed image that his mind sets. Jamai, by her very appearance, had just shattered that illusion. Her seventeen-year-old figure was very well endowed and not simply in those features natural to a mature woman. Muscle was evident in every sinewy movement, flowing beneath her luscious copper-toned skin. She could stand head-to-head with our tallest Elders.

But that costume. It appeared to be a variation of what she'd worn at the kiama a year ago. A snakeskin-print tank and trunks beneath a turquoise sleeveless waistcoat with wide, flaring collar flaps covered her torso. Her scuffed ankle boots were the same pair she'd worn when she saw me off to university nine months ago. The sun glistened across her skin, giving her a quite striking appearance.

"Kukuwazuka," I said, "we need to talk."

I made a sign to the Sacred Mountain before proceeding. She looked terrible. Scratches and welts covered her neck, limbs, and cheeks. Dark circles drooping to her cheekbones highlighted red-rimmed jade eyes. Yet the geothermal vents that powered our village never smoldered so much as the hurt in her stare. As I said... striking.

Speaking of which...

The next thing I remembered was Father shaking me back to consciousness. "Apparently it didn't go well," he commented. I shook off his arm and staggered to my feet. The breeze rustled through waist-high grasses and thorn bushes trimmed weekly by obedient mahutis. From horizon to horizon, not a figure stirred.

I wrenched from my slacks the wafer-thin compact that held the information I'd come 300 kilometers to deliver... truth she'd waited all her life to hear. I cinched the flap closed and stuffed it back in my hip pouch. "It's time we paid our respects to her father," I said. "This has gone on long enough."

"I know what you intend," Father said, "but you may find little support in the Council for your position. Some of my brothers have long perceived Jamai as a pox on our village."

I smirked at his ironic tone. "Don't worry, Father. Sometimes, it doesn't take a village."

AFTER MY ADVENTURES IN OLD NAIROBI, I began to understand what Jamai had told me at the rail station in Kibarenge on the day I departed for university. Before then, I could scarcely credit the issues she hinted at, the tales she told about these so-called "Children of Sydelle".

"Do you ever wonder why I didn't just ask the East African database to call up whatever information it had on my mother?" she said, holding my hands as ozone billowed around the snub-nosed pod waiting on its rail. "Not that I hadn't tried, but how do you begin a search without even a name to start with? I can't tell you how many times I've ransacked Baba's belongings," she sighed while the mountains behind us remained shrouded in morning mists. "Even his journals are blank. I can't find a copy of my own birth record. It's like he deliberately tried to wipe every trace of Mama out of existence. Why would he do that?"

I didn't have an answer then, not even a goodbye kiss, damn my heart. But I'd have something definite to search for now, and the means to do it. I'd keep her sad entreating gaze in every thought. Here and now, as Baba and I called on Mzee Dlamini, I suspected there was a more concrete rationale for his silence.

Siboniso Dlamini greeted us at the door. We exchanged muted "jambos" and settled in his receiving room, where the lamplight was also muted. The decorations were more Spartan than usual, as though he were determined to heap sackcloth and ashes on himself. The hardwood bench where we were seated followed the curvature of the wall. The casual conversation seemed to unnerve us all.

"I had to do it," he said at last. "She'd been eager for her initiation since she was a small *toto*. Once her name was engraved on our records, they would be watching. After last season's kiama, I knew the Children of Sydelle would come for her. Don't stare at me like that! You know they'd been searching for a daughter of Elias; Ngai alone knows why. In the forest, she can vanish like a phantom. Even I don't know where she could be. They can't find her… and Ngai forbid that they should."

I pondered whether or not I should tell him about our encounter that afternoon. The bruise still pulsing around my right eye ought to have been a clue. Mzee Dlamini's words ended in great racking sobs. Father guessed my dilemma and subtly shook his head.

The fuming accusations simmered, still in my chest. But while minutes passed as stones falling in a gourd, the temper subsided. "You can't understand," Father whispered to me, "what it is to lose a daughter. Or a son."

I nodded with bowed head. "Whatever your intentions, great Elder," I said through gritted teeth. I disliked this stupid parable-speak, but tradition demands that we address our Elders that way. "The spear is already at our throats. Let me tell you what I've learned of the owl who struts in our midst."

Mzee Dlamini dabbed his eyes as we presented our findings. He sat straighter as we droned on; his mouth tightened into a scowl. Jamai would have said that Ngai himself had restored the steel to his spine. All that was certain was that before I'd finished outlining our plan, the glaze had cleared from his sight.

"When shall we cast the first… oh, to hell with this proverbalizing. I'm on board! When do we act?"

"Tonight," I smiled. I'd been waiting all my life for someone to say that. "It'll be the Harvest Celebration. We've had a successful planting, so Father tells me. All our people will be there. More importantly the Elders will come in all their finery (no offense, great Elder) to offer libation speeches. Including the jackal in question. There'll be many opportunities to root the cur from among us."

"Well said," Mzee Dlamini agreed. "You may expect me eagerly."

As Father and I were leaving, Mzee Dlamini beckoned to me, addressing my father by name. "Wait, Lazaro, let the young man stay. I have something of great import to tell."

With a last curious glance, Father nodded and ducked out of the gloomy dwelling. I in turn resumed my seat while we faced each other in equally awkward postures.

"There is more you need to know, a story only I can tell you now." There was no excessive pride in this declaration; it seemed more of a resignation to forces beyond our understanding.

"I know you weren't responsible for Shin's death. But it comes back to that white dog, Auflauring. I didn't recognize him at the hearing. I'd been more concerned with Molefe's rants. Jamai had told me afterward what he was, but I had to pretend ignorance until I could speak privately with the magistrate. You see I'd met the man before, many years ago. We had both aged considerably since then. Let me tell you how this was so."

They set the firepods in the pit for the evening festivities. Though they had the appearance of corded logs, this was pure aesthetics. A geothermal vent lay two meters down at the bottom of the pit. Once the vent's shutters were opened, the heat of our mother planet would ignite, but not consume, the peculiar metal of the pods, giving both warmth and heat. Once they cooled, the pods could be stowed in the Communal Hall's cellar for future ceremonies. In this way our Elders embraced the future and honored the past.

Those thoughts seemed somehow mechanical on this, the 501st anniversary of our village's founding. There was much that was unknown about those chaotic times and much that Jamai had hinted at before our forced parting. We'd promised each other, after her initiation rites, that we'd share all that we knew. Of that, I gathered, she'd learned considerable.

I'd been keeping a lookout for her through the upper floor window of my family's loft. Her musky scent still lingered on the pillows from the time she stayed with us a year earlier. As far as I knew she and her father had been reconciled, but they were no longer as close as they'd always been.

She'd been the first to greet me after the boys from my age group returned from our rites. It's an archaic ritual; still, it provided an adhesive between generations. Father had peeled Jamai off me only with excessive force. Even then he'd been apologetic, inviting her, and her father, naturally, to the grand celebration that followed.

I didn't care. At the dance following the ceremony, I kept her close to my side, and I don't think she minded. God, she danced like a goddess freed of her chains. No one objected then; it was my night and she was my choice. What were they going to do about it?

The xylophone band and Jamaican troubadours, live from a Caribbean sat-link, had seemed all too excessive. I'd borne it with manly dignity, though I could've curled up and died from embarrassment. But I was my parents' last living offspring, and there was the bright joy in their tears. For them I could bear a little personal discomfit.

That had been the week before I'd gone to study at Old Nairobi. Before I found Li Shun Kim, and the police found what was left of him.

"You should be resting." Father's bulbous head appeared in the passageway from downstairs.

A nervous force kept me rooted to the window overlooking our village. "I'd had more than enough rest in the grand suites if His Royal Magistrate," I smirked. Even this was forced mirth.

The aeroform mattress crinkled under Father's weight as he settled on a corner of the bed. I sensed an inhalation, but the expected proverb didn't emerge quickly enough. "Father?"

"We never talk about Goukoni," he said. "We searched for your brother for over a year, but there was never a trace. Your mother couldn't live without the sound of children laughing in the house. Imagine when S'manga announced that you and Ahela would be twins. And when your sister vanished, in the same area, at the same age as when your brother... you said, at the time... you said you'd felt..."

"It was an empathic response," I replied, a bit too sharply, and apologized at once. "I didn't lie about that, Father. Not about her murder."

The exhalation came. Not the casual "humm" such comments usually engendered. This was a drawn-out exhausted affair of acceptance. There'd always been hope, at least in my parents' eyes. Ahela's body had never been recovered. After the evidence Jomoro collected at Dobra Damo... damn! "Have they found her?"

"No. Ngai grant that we never do."

"Father, what exactly happened to Goukoni?"

He didn't answer right away. When I glanced over one shoulder he appeared rooted in stone on the bed. "Forget it," I blurted. "It's not my place…"

"As parents," Father announced, "we're forced to make difficult choices when it's in the best interests of our children. Especially when you are the only living offspring." His glance met mine, sharply, then darted away.

"Jamai had been a good substitute for Ahela, especially as the two of them were so close in age. It did wonders for your mother to care for her when her father was on his frequent horticultural outings. But we'd lost too much to those diseased parasites, your older brother and your sister. When we were told you were apprehended… of course the charges were blatantly false, we knew that, but when we learned that poor Asian's name… there was nothing more we could do for her while she remained in Baba Elgonyi. We had to consider the safety of our people as a whole."

"*Had*?" I said. I left the window, crossing the floor to stand over him. "*Was*? Always past tense."

"Son…"

"You knew what Siboniso Dlamini was going to do."

Father surged to his feet. "God damn it, what did you expect us to do? Your mother cried for two nights when Jomoro contacted us. I can't do this to your mother again. Do you know what the penalty for…? Damn it, I don't have to explain this. She's not our daughter!"

"Not? What difference can that make? After what she did for Mother, how could you even think of…"

"Don't you throw that in my face!"

"Lazaro!" Mother's voice shrieked from below. "Lazaro, come down here this instant."

Father and I faced each other, trembling with equal fervor. I looked away first. He backed up a few steps, then stormed to the passageway without a word.

We ate the evening meal in silence. Our tempers had cooled. Mother's meal was exquisite as always, and so we told her. For each other, Father and I had nothing more to say that night.

FOR DAYS ELDERS HAD BEEN GATHERING beneath the sacred baobab where our grandfather Benjamin Dlamini had been buried four centuries earlier. These were the Prodigal sons of Baba Elgonyi, men who had been boys that found new lives in Kigali, Nakura, Juba, and elsewhere. Many were accompanied by their smiling brides. Every visitor's arrival was recorded by a short, stubby Anubis-headed mahuti that directed them to follow the lighted path through the market to the village square.

Pembo had been brewing in private vats for weeks for this evening's celebration. Certain young men pranced among the girl-folk playing sweet harmonies on their flutes. Others competed with drums slung to their hips, some boys nudging themselves around the cairn of fire jetting into the square.

The Elders joined in a collective laugh, some slapping calabashes mounted on their knees. Massive twitches jerked my muscles, demanding that we stand and be done with this. A sidelong glance from Father quelled those urges. This was the young men's hour; it wasn't my place to spoil it just yet.

One by one, the Council of Elders for Baba Elgonyi praised the accomplishments of the previous spring's harvest, and those of our young people who'd placed among the top ranks of Upper School bands and choirs. This went on for another interminable hour, most of their words forgotten in the events to come. When the time for the libation blessing came, the impulse became too strong to ignore.

As Odu Molefe lifted his arms, I vaulted to my feet. The words Molefe would have spoken escaped as wisps of smoke from his nostrils. Good. As satisfying as it'd have been to smash his nostrils into his nasal cavities, I'd be just as content to roll him beneath the wheels of the law.

"Peace, Grandfathers," I said. "Before we proceed with the libation, one issue more must be brought before the kiama."

Molefe's owlish gaze narrowed. He responded in neutral tones. "This matter may be addressed at the proper time and place."

"I say we hear it now," Mzee Dlamini growled.

"I too would like to hear this," Father chimed. "After all, we are assembled. We may hear and dispense with the formalities appropriately." The rest of the kiama, though befuddled by this interruption, agreed with many inclinations of their shaven heads.

Everyone resumed their seats. "Grandfathers, listen," I said. "I have a story to tell. A young woman betrothed herself to one of our most promising Elders. She came to our village possessing extraordinary gifts. On her back she bore the symbol of a scholarly sect, little known, which a certain member of this gathering felt compelled to investigate.

"Like so many before, this person discovered few concrete details about this sect, other than it involved the accumulation of arcane knowledge of the psyche, which had once brought disaster on one of its own. As a student of history, one could see danger in this woman's association. Our people had undergone two centuries of barbarism following the colonial period. Might this woman not present a similar threat?

"He watched her carefully, making no secret of his distrust. In time this woman was in childbirth. It was a difficult labor. Finally, this Elder was approached by that sect that opposed hers. They offered a proposal: delay medical aid for one hour, until they could assemble a team to spirit her and her offspring away. The child would be cared for, and no one would be wiser.

"But something had gone wrong. Either they never assembled the promised team, or more likely they betrayed his trust. In any event help came too late to save the woman's life. That guilt has lain as a shroud on his crown."

I paused. Hmm, not bad. I might have a talent for dissembling, if a future in architectural design didn't pan out.

"What could he do?" I continued. "He could never redress this wrong. The only viable option was to watch the child and be certain she never learned the truth of her birthright. He discovered to his horror that the child's abilities exceeded those of her mother. Worse, subconsciously the hostility he'd harbored for the parent had been transferred to the child.

"In time, he contrived a scheme. Together, he and the child's father agreed that withholding the truth was the only sure way to protect her from the evil lying in wait for her."

To my right Mzee Dlamini turned aside as I spoke. To every point thus far he had nodded in fuming silence. Meanwhile he maintained a silent vigil with her unseen opponents. The girl was steeped in tradition, which was the foundation of her well-being. By tradition she was bound to avenge her mother's death, but only if she knew the circumstances behind the event.

"Last season the unthinkable happened. His sons rushed home to report that this child had assaulted his youngest daughter, the most precious possession of his life. Though the accusation was proven false, his associates deemed it time to weed out this bitter seed. Under the guise of a kiama, he tried to have her committed to an institute operating under the auspices of his associates, the so-called Children of Sydelle.

"He tried, and he failed, because Jamai Fatima Dlamini also had allies, among them his eldest daughter. Only one course was left open. He had to wipe Jamai Dlamini out of existence. Statistically at least, this was done. A program was implanted in the community database, and on a prescribed date — by coincidence, her own birthday — all her personal records were blotted from the East African Community's localized databases. All, that is, but one."

If a hyena had ever smiled with closed lips, Molefe would have mastered the skill. "You can prove none of this," he said. "Do you expect these revered Elders to believe I'd done these things?"

"Had I said it was you that I referred to?" I asked innocently.

The smile reversed. "You have no proof…"

Actually, nestled in my waist pouch was all the proof necessary. I extracted that and tossed it at the Elder's feet.

Mzee Dlamini grabbed the cube and examined it front to back, side to side. "An Invasive Instructive Filter," he growled. He pitched this outside the cairn of stones encompassing the ceremonial fire and started towards Molefe.

Father and I restrained him. "Not yet," I whispered. "Let's tighten the noose a little more." Mzee Dlamini flushed with wrath, but held his ground.

I collected the IIF from the dirt and extended it toward each Elder in turn. Once they'd all had an opportunity to examine it, I snapped the cube into my fist. "Five centuries ago they called these pernicious things *viruses*, an anthropomorphism referring to their ability to multiply voraciously once they infected a data stream. It's not always possible even today to shield databases from their influence. This specimen managed to infiltrate every machine in the Community's data grid before its activation. Fortunately, the defensive filters at the EAC's Central Database are well fortified. They captured this program probing at the Central Database's firewall and analyzed it within days of its interception."

"A heinous act," Molefe conceded. While his features practiced remorse, his hands kneaded the lion's head knob on his staff knuckle-white. A sheen of perspiration glowed bright on his face in the firelight. "But this is all circumstantial."

"Indeed," I agreed. Turning to a space behind the Elders, I whistled to my former captor. A dark hulk of a man in short sleeved khakis and trunks sidled into the circle of Elders. "Magistrate, if you will. I believe you have more concrete evidence to present us."

Jomoro Al-Amain's fist clutched the handle of the curved blade riding across his waist. By the light of the firepods, his front teeth, chipped to blunt tips, projected impatiently over his lower lip. He inclined his brow, then faced Molefe sternly as he began his presentation.

"Mzee Molefe, several weeks ago we initiated a tap on your private communiqués, based on suspicions raised by parties I am not yet at liberty to disclose. It appears, Grand Elder, you've maintained a healthy correspondence with the director of the Dobra Damo Institute for Mental Health. Our investigations have concluded that facility was in fact a front, a cell for the collective known as the *Children of Sydelle*."

Agitated murmurs coursed through the ranks of Elders and the spectators who'd begun to gather in the square. Several times I overheard anxious queries, usually having to do with the identity or motives of this group. Jomoro proceeded to supply the answers.

"For many years, we have been aware of the consistent disappearance of children from outlying settlements of our district. In collaboration with my brother magistrates, we have coordinated our investigations and uncovered a disturbing pattern of kidnapping. These missing *totos* were rarely found, until recently. Two weeks ago, accompanied by young Mr. Hadebe, we served a warrant on Dobra Damo, where we encountered stiff resistance. A double dose of anesthesene gas was necessary to subdue the facility's defenders. The subsequent search yielded a series of catacombs. These contained the bodies of several dozen youths between the ages of seven and thirteen. Their bodies were preserved in a hard, chitinous material similar to amber. Every one of them had suffered from catastrophic nervous system failure. We have catalogued ninety-seven *totos* and matched their remains to those on the missing list via genetic identification."

"Your consultant at Ms. Dlamini's kiama, Bren Auflauring, vanished shortly before the raid," I added, standing over Molefe. "Our Magistrate's sources have identified him as a false priest of that cell of the Children of Sydelle."

Jomoro glowered, clearly unwilling to share the spotlight. "We have you as an accessory to murder, multiple counts of child abuse and falsification of public records. Come with me, you're under arrest."

As Jomoro reached for his arm, a fit of trembling seized Molefe's limbs. He jerked from the magistrate's touch like a skittish wuolo dog and scrambled around the outer ring of Elders, who appeared stunned into immobility. "You stupid child!" he shrieked. "Do you know what you've done? They'll kill us all!"

Apprehension tightened in my chest. Jamai had said he'd been afraid of her at the kiama, but clearly he feared something far more substantial. Molefe bolted from the square, with Mzee

Dlamini and I pelting at his heels. Jomoro followed, bellowing for him to halt *in the name of the law* or some such nonsense.

For a man in his early 50s, he put quite a distance between us. People lurched from his path out of deference to his high office, clearing the way from the celebration. Molefe dodged between barrels of pembo with surprising ease in the now-deserted market, rushing along a wide lane between dwellings before he was stopped. Sadly, it wasn't by us.

A mound of surprisingly perfect circumference roiled from beneath the outer wall of Baba Elgonyi. The pimple of earth undulated in our direction, plowing a neat path below Odu Molefe's feet.

As he tumbled face-forward, the earth surged, cascading from the neck and shoulders of… Ngai knew what the bloody hell it was! A narrow crest of bristles ran from brow to shoulder. Its square muzzle grinned hyena-like over its fallen prey. And it kept rising. Arms as wide as a drumhead heaved it from its burrow. Once on the surface, a knife-edged tail swished aside clods of soil.

Mzee Dlamini and I froze in its tree-like shadow, up until the moment it lunged at Molefe. I suppose nobody deserved to die that way, but the truth was we needed his help to round up the rest of his conspirators. We tossed gourds and stones at its impressive biceps while Jomoro snapped the other weapon he carried from the holster at his hip.

In one fluid movement, the Adjudicator in his fist flowed into position. In another age, it might appear to be a toy, with its massive barrel and massive grip. This *toy*, however, was attuned to its master's voice. As he took aim, Jomoro called, "Kihoro!"

One pellet sank juicily into the beast's 50-plus centimeter chest… just one. Its head and most of its upper chest vanished behind the fireball that followed. Flames sizzled past the rooftops and dissipated. The gourd I was about to pitch rolled clumsily from my hand. Its crest ducked down, sniffing the ashes drifting down its ribcage. Unfortunately, in all respects it appeared unharmed. Rising from its crouch, the beast grumbled, "Don't bother me."

Its arm whooshed, dashing both of us into the walls of the nearest homestead. Jomoro's body clattered among the shattered carts of the vegetable growers. Carts, poles! Yes! The marketplace vendors pegged their carts into preset slots in the jade paving, using composite-mold piping such as those where Jomoro floundered. Those pipes had greater tensile strength and density than forged steel. They'd make a fine weapon in a clutch, which we certainly were in now.

Hwenge skidded on his heels five meters from the scene, but he actually sidled back a few paces at the sight of his father's assailant. I smacked his shoulder and jabbed a finger toward the pipes at our feet. Not waiting for his support, I grabbed for one, a substantially heavier item than I expected, and swung at our invader's bowed head.

Other bodies streaked past us in panicked flight, many of them matrons bundling squalling *totos* to their breasts. Hands reached around me, grasping at posts, a sign that my kinsmen had risen to the occasion. A soft breeze wafted past our quarry, carrying with it the stench of fresh-turned earth and soured blood.

Shrieking like enraged hyenas, we threw ourselves as one body at the invader. Oh, we beat a meaty tom-tom across its backside, and we left a series of impressive indentations in its flesh… briefly. Muscle rippled and the blows healed. We ought to have been so fortunate.

Its arms lashed out like trees, and with each swing another man cried out. My friends piled onto conical rooftops and thumped onto power generators. Every blow swept us aside as easily as straw dolls. Hwenge's hips bashed into an upturned cart of netting. I ducked beneath another savage swipe, assumed a proper defensive stance… and found myself alone.

Breath steamed on a huff gushing from the beast's muzzle, wet with Molefe's juices. We circled the market area while its peeled-back chops exposed rows of serrated teeth. Siboniso Dlamini padded around to its rear, cradling a shock pistol. That distraction was all I needed. I brought the post down on the beast's skull with all my strength.

The ceramic burst into pieces with a crack of thunder, after which the creature shook its mane and leered down at me. Its paw came at me on a rush of wind. I sprung back to escape the attack. At least that feeble maneuver deflected the blow enough that I only tumbled onto an overturned cart.

An electric blue energy streak thrummed into the fisi-faced bastard. It crouched, paw drawn over its muzzle, huffing with deeper and deeper rumbles of thunder. Mzee Dlamini stepped into its circle of arms, shock pistol extended, probably in hopes of finishing the job.

A sharp upward thrust knocked him into my legs just as I was getting them back beneath me. It nudged the fallen pistol, a useful tool against a garden-variety criminal, and flicked its big toe. It caught the pistol in one great ham and squeezed. There was no shriek of metal, no crinkle of delicate focusing lenses. The thing simply opened its palm. Pieces of pistol tinkled to the paving.

"All things die," it philosophized. "Tonight it begins with you."

You Westerners have an inflated notion of heroism. No doubt you'd expect me to strike a bold pose and rain defiant curses on the villain. Bloody hell! Every joint in my body shrieked in their sockets. I could barely draw a breath; my chest stung like a nest of wasps had had their way with me. As that thing loomed over us, I threw myself over Mzee Dlamini.

At that moment, a burgundy pair of thighs flashed between us. A lion's roar shuddered through the square. Stones and dirt clods sprayed skyward as the oversized brute's body ground through the paving. The wall of Mzee Rabai's pharmacy stopped its backward flight.

Jamai still shielded her father and me, hands spread wide before her. Her deltoids rose like two shields bracing her shoulders, the trapezius flexed across her back. Her auburn curls billowed on the surge of power coursing through her. I'd hoped that she would come. I'd wanted her to witness Odu Molefe's humiliation after all the years of torment he'd heaped on her. Perhaps in my arrogance I even assumed she would follow me like a phantom into the village and, just as in the old days, we could share our adventures over the past few months. Clearly that hope had also gone awry.

She glanced over her shoulder, the whites of her eyes glimmering as twin moons. She stormed along the trench that the creature's body had dug, to stand huffing over it.

"Lepidopteran," its voice slurred, seeming to rumble from the Earth's depths. "I have been waiting for you."

"I'm sorry to have detained you," she replied impatiently. She grabbed a handful of mane and filled her other hand with a mass of scruff from its back.

S'manga Nlebela had said Jamai could do practically anything, but that had just been words. The veins pulsed in her biceps as she heaved. Grunting, she heaved the creature, a child lifting an ape. She pivoted on both heels and bashed its skull a meter deep into the pharmacy wall. Masonry tinkled to the ground as she wrenched it free and jammed its face in the wall again. She backpedaled fast when it took a swing at her. The air whistled as its arms lashed through empty space. Jamai bounced back another step; then she bent at the waist and pushed off. Her heels slapped on its back and pushed off again, bouncing once after landing behind her opponent.

A massive puff of steam gushed in the night air, dispersing to all sides as it advanced. She ducked beneath its next swing and stepped to one side. Her left arm stretched forth, and an Elder's staff whooshed across the square into her waiting palm, and from there right into the creature's midsection.

Incredibly the beast buckled. With an upward crack, the staff snapped into its jaw, making a return sweep to the belly on the way down. Once she tossed the staff aside, however, it fell to the ground as sawdust and splinters.

Under the moonlight, a sheen of perspiration shone on her skin. Jamai hyperventilated as she stood over that thing, her thighs trembling. Its eyes now seemed blurred with confusion. Her husky voice cracked as she spoke. "Tell your masters they're not welcome here. This is not a request, and it is not negotiable. Lay a hand on my father again, and I promise, I'll feed you your eyes."

She gestured to the fields west of our village as the creature shifted to a sitting position. "Be somewhere else," she said. "You don't belong here."

"Neither do you," it exhaled. Nevertheless, it rose, until the tips of its nipples hung over the tips of her eyelashes. A faint vibration rattled through our toes as the earth opened and swallowed it. Stones clattered into the tunnel it had opened long after the beast had gone.

Kalila Maji already had a wash-pan and damp cloth in hand as Jamai eased to one knee beside her father. Kalila passed her the cloth, which Jamai dipped in the pan with a soft "asante". Mzee Dlamini clutched her wrists, and she flinched. But tears stained both their faces.

"Samahani, *toto*, samahani," he whispered. "It was the only way to protect you. I couldn't…"

"Shh," she said, dabbing his brow as her father continued babbling.

"Beautiful," he said. "Just like your mother."

I'm afraid the tenderness of the moment had been lost on me. "What the bloody hell was that thing?" I demanded.

She ignored the question, which only inflamed me more. Still, her father grasped the import of my words, even if I hadn't. Grasping her hand, Mzee Dlamini spoke with sudden firmness. "You have to leave. Now." Over her protestations, he rasped, "I'm not important, it's you they want. They'll know you've been here. Go! Go quickly! Please, do as I say, for your mother's sake."

The wet cloth splattered into the pan. Trembling fingers curled and rose to her mouth. On the far side of the square, Jomoro Al-Amain was trying to shake off a covey of female admirers, and I realized she had another good reason to flee. "Listen to your father," I said. "The magistrate is coming for you!"

Jamai spared me an emerald glare. She wrapped her father in a python-like embrace. Kalila Maji received a brief hug also. Then she scrambled to one side and bolted through the center of the now-quiescent revelers, who parted for her like the Red Sea.

I just managed to knock Jomoro's cannon upward as he took aim at her back. Moments later she'd vanished into the night. "Have you lost your senses?" Jomoro roared. "Don't you realize the danger she is in?"

"She saved all our lives!" I started to protest, but authorities have always had a way of shouting when you're trying to communicate with them.

"The plan was to take her into custody for her own safety," he said, "before the Children of Sydelle did. How the bloody hell am I supposed to protect her when I don't know where the fuck she is?"

Day Two: Sins Imposed on the Innocent

PERSUADING JOMORO TO LET ME PURSUE JAMAI was a good deal easier than we had any business to expect. Father insisted that I was under legal obligation to bring Jamai in, since my "absurd" charges were tied to hers. Also, he pointed out, my personal feelings shouldn't allow me to leave Jamai alone and starving in the wilderness.

Jomoro, in turn, bitched and huffed, matching Father's steady glare without blinking. I looked across their overarching stares and told them I had an emotional advantage over her that the Poppy Girls in question hadn't. Granted, this was still only theory on my part, not subject to scientific scrutiny. I had great confidence in my belief, however. Besides, where Jamai was concerned one really couldn't assume anything.

As a precautionary measure, Jomoro's deputies attached a geostationary tag to my skiff, stressing the seriousness of the consequences we would both face should I fail to retrieve her. Not to mention the dishonor I'd bring down on my family for generations to come.

"In that event," Jomoro insisted, referring to my imminent failure, "this will no longer be my problem. And I assure you, the East African Community's Rangers will be far less lenient on her than I would."

I'd have help. That neuroplagic blob on her hand wasn't just an access port for data retrieval. It might also be used as a personal tag by the authorities to track and apprehend suspects on the lam, once they obtained the proper warrants, of course. That gnawing apprehension in my stomach wasn't relieved by Jomoro telling me that.

He hadn't used the thing sooner to track Jamai, he explained, on account of Odu Molefe's erasure of her statistical data from the EAC's mainframes. Her linkup's signature frequency had to be rooted out from their protected archives and downloaded to us.

I carried that signature in the motherboard of my father's skiff. It was triangulating her location now via the EAC's geostationary platform, using Baba Elgonyi as a base coordinate. Until a directional pointer could be downloaded into the skiff's motherboard, all I could do was park on the savannah and wait.

I put the interminable wait to good use in a data search for any references to "Ngojama". Jamai had spoken about it before our parting nine months earlier. The best I could conjure was an early 20th Century text file from late Colonial times, by a white researcher bearing all the prejudices of her kind. The text described something very much like our intruder, a monster that struck bewildered travelers with a nail embedded in its palm and drank their blood.

Pity I wasn't able to attend Molefe's autopsy, not that there was much left of him to examine. Cross-referencing within the same series of text-files suggested a link with the Jinn of Semitic lore. By exploring that angle, I thought I uncovered a possible defense. "Voiceprint," I said, rotating my wrist as I dictated to the initializer in my hand. "Store the enclosed image in primary memory. Display when I and I alone say the following prompt..."

My model was of a different variety than hers. While her wrist comp was more decorative, at least mine was not so obtrusive. The initializer was inset in a natural cavity between my first and second knuckle, and only surfaced when given a short code word of my choosing. The fact that my initializer was the size of a flea was also helpful.

In the darkness before dawn, the skiff's onboard map finally projected a hand-sized image of the local terrain, with a pink arrow pointing west, away from Baba Elgonyi. The skiff buffed across the roughshod ground in the indicated direction.

For approximately thirty minutes, trees and outcroppings whooshed past the sunroof as a steady "twoop" guided me on my travels. But a half hour past sunrise, the signal vanished. It did not slowly fizzle or fight bravely to maintain signal integrity before fading. It simply disappeared in mid-twoop!

As I said, help was available. The question was, did I want it? Had I reported this to Jomoro, the matter would have been referred to the District Police. Friend that he was on other issues, Jomoro was neither an imaginative nor a flexible man. Once she was taken into custody, assuming that was even possible, Jamai would never have the chance to tell her side of the story. For that reason alone, I had to find her first. I had to know the truth.

At nine a.m. her signal resumed, eleven kilometers to the north. How in bloody hell was that possible? Another eleven kilometers on top of the two she'd run after leaving Baba Elgonyi? Nobody had that kind of endurance, unless she had help too. Probably sleeping with the snakes again. I tabbed the ignition stud and steered the skiff in the direction of the onboard arrow.

The odd thing was how intermittent the signal was. Faint also, as though it were coming from underground. I pushed the skiff perhaps too close to its safety limits, but I had no choice. She appeared to be moving at breakneck pace. The arrows suggested she was taking a zigzag course, generally west for a good twenty minutes. Then the signal froze in one spot on the tracking screen. Good, now it held steady and strong. I shifted the skiff to its highest speed.

It was probably momentum alone that saved me. Vines surged from the ground, spraying clods as they clawed at the skiff. Finger-length thorns shrieked over the chassis. Sheer velocity tore most of them from their roots, but they kept twitching for several moments before falling away. I was only able to evade those snapping vines by a great deal of hazardous swerving.

My crazy driving raised quite a dust cloud, which probably obscured the other apes charging at the skiff. Oh they were men, but with huge blobby arms and thighs, veins mounted high on every muscle as though they'd indulged too much in muscle enhancers. They must have planted those vines to ensnare Jamai; they caught me instead.

I swerved the skiff at a furious clip as they stumbled in my wake. Several came close enough to swat at the propulsion pods with their fist-sized bracelets. Their bald pates almost blinded me as the late morning sun glinted off their heads. Scimitar-like blades snipped from the bracelets, shrieking across the chassis. Fortunately, none of them connected with me. I steered in erratic circles through their mass before I was able to break away. I'd never seen their like before, but I guessed they served that phantom bitch Sydelle that Jamai had told me about.

I'm not sure what happened next. The apes stormed toward their own skiffs, screaming oaths. One of them seemed to be sucked into the Earth, vehicle and all. A black mound roiled beneath them while a stiff ruff pushed to the surface. A skiff tilted onto its pods. I didn't stay to watch what was sure to be a massacre, but circled back along the path of Jamai's signal.

There wasn't much opportunity to give praise to the Almighty for my luck. It'd dawned on me that once the thing was finished with Sydelle's shaven apes, it would be driving that earthen mound towards me. It seemed a good time to put my insensible plan to work.

I brought the skiff to a grinding halt. Father was going to hate me for this, but I switched the Entertainment module to stand-alone mode and disconnected it from the motherboard.

I'd already loaded the image I needed. Ngai pray that the module's tiny projectors would be sufficient for the job.

Dust rose and screams echoed distantly as I set the module onto a rutted stone jutting from the plains. I fixed it in place with adhesive strips, then programmed the angle of the projection beams to the left and right at 45 degrees each. I directed the final beam straight to the ground. I glanced up, and the sweat dimpled in my armpits.

Half a kilometer away the mound shifted, a grinding dot looming larger by the second. I hunched by the passenger-side fuel pod and called out my prompt, "Elias!"

Three violet beams glowed from the module, harmless in themselves. It was the image they formed that mattered. Three five-pointed stars, each within their own flaming circle, appeared in Ngojama's path. I didn't share that freak's convictions, but I'd take any weapons I could find.

The star that pointed at the ground rippled and bent as the mound slowed beneath it, and stopped. Dirt dribbled off the heap of fresh-turned earth. I gritted my teeth till they ached, my breath hot in my lungs. Well, the mound remained stationary, and nothing was surging out from it. That could mean anything, but I'd assume Ngojama was stymied, for now. I exhaled, sprang back into the pilot's seat and resumed my tracking.

A cinnamon heap rose out from the crackling grass. My chest still reeked of perspiration and my heart thudded against my breastbone. I'd barely managed to steady my breathing after the past few minutes' misadventures when this new sight set me to panting like a rheumatic jackass again.

The skiff's propulsion pods scraped Earth as it skid to a halt. Jamai lay dusted with loose soil, looking for all the world as though she were asleep. Head turned to one side, cheek nestled to the upturned dirt, her arms were buried to the shoulders in the embracing Earth. Like... like that Poppy Girl I'd found outside the Molefe's household the year before.

I barely remembered darting over the skiff's door. She was limp as I dragged her hips from the embracing Earth. She coughed fitfully, and I exhaled. Dust still clouded the area a few kilometers back where Sydelle's apes had fallen.

That didn't matter. Everything would be fine. We could go home now. Her eyelids blinked, beating softly as butterfly wings. I met her glazed stare with a smile. "*Habari yako, Kukuwazuka,*" I said. "How are you feeling?"

She punched me in the mouth.

I managed one stumbling step back while flashes burst over my eyes. She kept coming, her fists raining on my upraised arms, back, anywhere that was exposed. Her arms were flying too swiftly for me to grasp. All the while she screamed, "You stupid fisi! Where the hell were you? You left me to die! You goddamned son of a bitch, I waited for you! I waited and you never came! Damn you to hell, why did you come back?"

I caught her wrists, finally, and held on while she threatened to wrench both our arms from our sockets. Tempting as it was, I wasn't going to strike her. "Stop it! Stop it, you'll hurt yourself!" I insisted. "I'm here now! If you'd talk to me..."

"Hah! What good would that do? You, the great chief's son, overawing the Elders with your deeds."

Her words and the bitterness behind them, hit me like a cold slap. "What's the matter with you?" I stammered. "Everything that's happened in the past few months I've done for you. We said we'd walk through hell for each other, do you remember that? You said I was yours, flesh, blood, and spirit. We both said it."

"I can't go back," she retorted. "Why can't you understand that? Too much has happened. I… I can't wrap my mind around everything that's gone wrong."

"We can fix this. If you'd only talk to your father, we could sort this out. Your records can be restored. Odu Molefe can't hurt us anymore."

She wrenched herself free of my sweaty hands. She didn't run away again, but her limbs remained as tight as drumheads. "My father is the one who left me out here," she said in a strained voice. She padded a few steps toward the tree line, then swung back in the general direction of Baba Elgonyi. "Why did you do this to me?" she shrieked. "I hate you! I hate you!" Her voice croaked partway into her next accusation. What she hacked out was, "Damn you, I love you, Baba! Why can't I hate you…?"

Her back was to me, stiff as the towers of the EAC Governing House. Sniffles were plainly audible, but she tried to convey the illusion of strength. "You have to go back, Rafiki. There's nothing you can do for me. I've brought too much shame on my father already. Besides, what difference would it make if my records were restored? Can you petition the kiama to sanction an initiation?"

"What are you talking about?"

Still facing away, she snapped, "I never had my initiation. I'm not part of your tribe. I'm not part of my own family. I never will be. May fleas devour your eyes, I don't exist!"

The entire planet shifted to one side. My legs seemed to stand on a lopsided plane. "But… he promised… this was the season you were going to… Jamai, that's obscene!"

She started to laugh, and not a harmless or even a scornful laugh. The high tingle in her giggles smacked of madness. "You don't… you don't believe in such anachronistic balderdash.

You told me after you... shit, shit, shit. They just didn't want crazy old me in their clique."

I swung her around and shrieked incoherent nothings at her, shaking her as though that might solve anything. When I couldn't stare into her stricken face any longer, I held her close, not speaking all the random thoughts coalescing into nauseous pinpricks.

Father didn't tell me. He had to know what Mzee Dlamini had done, and he couldn't... wouldn't tell me. If it'd been a simple matter of reinstating her records... I couldn't bring her back. What would she have to go back to? If that other story about the Poppy Girls was true, she had nothing ahead of her but a lifetime in prison.

Her body trembled in my grip, her arms loose at her sides, chin nuzzling my shoulder. I didn't know what else to do, except to stand and hold her while the sun crept behind the Sacred Mountain.

THE FIRST THING I DID WAS TO RAID THE SKIFF'S COMM BOARD and weave the spare parts into a sort of smoke screen. This I bundled into a grease rag and knotted over Jamai's wrist comp. In theory, the crude electromagnetic field generated by my cock-up rig ought to diffuse any tracking signals such as the one I'd used to find her.

"I don't know what to do," I admitted. "Jomoro made it clear that I faced a stiff prison term if I failed him."

Jamai rubbed the wrist I'd bound in my rig with a frown. "You? Based on what? What could he possibly expect to incarcerate you for?"

"The charge would be murder in the first degree."

Her arms dropped to her sides. She started to mouth several things, none of which seemed to reach past the muddle in her brain. Her head started to shake, and I'd have listened to any of those cracks over the return of that mad laugh. "No!" she croaked. "No, that's not... No! That's a lie! A murderer? You? I can believe many things, but never that!"

In spite of the monsoon torrent of events, that faith warmed me. "So you're the only one capable of murder, is that so? I don't believe that about you, either. Whatever happened, it has to be a mistake."

"Get out." She clapped her hands over her ears and marched for the distant trees. Fortunately, my legs were longer and fitter than her muscle-bound thighs and easily kept pace. "*Kwenda nyumbani*! Go away!"

"I know you," I said to her back. "You'd get sick if an impala scratched itself on a thorn."

"Get out!"

"Oh no, I'm not leaving you alone, and what's more you can't make me leave."

"Yes I can," she tossed over her shoulder. Even so, she'd begun to slow.

"Ha! Bluster and snot! The day you'd hurt anyone..."

I don't know what she screamed at me. A harmattan wind whipped through her curls as she spun. Worse still, the psychic storm surging through her chewed a three-meter swath in the savannah, churning toward me.

Spasms jerked my legs, struggling against the automatic and sensible urge to run. I was barely able to stand by force of will while my muscles shouted no-no-no! Ngai be praised, my theory was borne out. A few meters short of where I trembled, the swath crackled with the violently disturbed Earth, dividing into two branches that plowed a comfortable two meters along my flanks.

The uprooting of sod and stone abruptly ceased. Jamai stood behind the settling reddish-brown dust, hand outstretched. Her mouth hung in a narrow ellipse, her jade eyes wide and moist. She sagged over her knees, all the energy drained out of her. Shaking her head, she gasped, "No… please go… please…"

"I'm not going to leave you alone," I repeated. I stepped around the trench her power just excavated and took her arm. "Your father could have never left you out here if you'd had any power over him. That's your weakness. You don't have any power over the ones you love."

She seemed to get her breath back. Standing tall, she stared down at her fumbling fingers. "Then we have a problem. You didn't really think I could toss Ngojama about like a cat's toy if he hadn't wished it? Maybe he was confused, or didn't understand. That so-called battle last night, Rafiki, was only a show. I was only trying to protect Baba."

"I'm not sure I like where this is going."

"Nor should you. Ngojama has been protecting me these past weeks. If he finds me with you tonight, he's liable to kill you."

"Kukuwazuka, don't tell me you like that thing!"

"What difference would it make if I did? Damn you, what choice did I have?" In spite of the firmness in her words, tears still flowed, no matter how I brushed them from her cheeks. "They tried to kill me! I didn't mean to… it's just… I don't have anybody else! The only ones I get on with are the dead. Who else did I have to care about?"

At dusk we reached the local geothermal station. During our ride, Jamai had been morose, silent. She'd had eyes only for the grass parting for her as we whisked through it.

One of forty such installations in the Nairobi District, this station was linked with the solar convection fields in Bengala and Zanj to form an indispensable power grid. Around the perimeter were scattered drill heads in cloth casings, abandoned either when a bore proved fruitless or the drill simply shattered.

Our skiff coasted to a rest outside a workman's shed. This would be unmanned as these facilities were largely automated via a geo-satellite control post in Nairobi. Jamai brushed her fingers over the blinking identi-slot in the door. With a jelly-like pop, the lock shot from the door in a short burst of sparks. Without a word, she breezed inside. I followed.

It wasn't much to look at. The shed's light cinnamon timbers were racked with shelves. These were filled to capacity with spare pumps, heat exchangers, tools (some of which I didn't recognize), and various other contrivances. The window on the right-hand wall could do with a good spraying to remove the oily residue and oversized fingerprints.

Jamai curled up on the bench facing the window while I divided the few nutrient bars I'd brought from home between us. Then I collected a welder's torch and cowl from the shelves and stepped back outside. Within a few minutes, I'd burned several five-pointed stars in the trees and drill heads, in an equidistant radius around the work shed. With any luck, they'd keep Ngojama at a comfortable distance.

When I stepped back inside, Jamai was still nibbling her first nutrient bar. I didn't expect much conversation this evening and hadn't planned to press her for any. She volunteered it nonetheless.

"I don't understand any of this," Jamai said. "Why would the police think you killed anyone?" She pressed her hand over mine. "Rafiki, who do they think you killed?"

This was going to be a difficult conversation in any event. I suppose the least painful option would be just to proceed. "I met Li Shun Kim in Nairobi. He was one of Elias' people."

I didn't think the name would mean anything to her. We met him only the one time, over ten years earlier. Nevertheless, it sparked instant recognition. "That nice old man at the Masai Mara museum?"

"Yes. You remember, he told us he owed your father his life. He never explained how. I thought he might have the answers you needed." I paused then. I'd have wished a thousand stones were piled on my grave not to have to say those things seething in my mind. Somehow my silence told her everything.

"He's dead, isn't he?"

"Yes. I couldn't do anything for him. How did you...?"

"I knew. I sensed it in the brooding yoke your spirit carries. It seems so much heavier than the one you usually carry. I always seem to know when the shadows are coming to carry men's souls away."

Hmmph. Most days getting her to talk was akin to forcing the Zambezi River to flow backwards. Apparently, I hadn't the same problem.

"I wanted to show you Nairobi," I told her as I passed over another nutrient bar. "The global floods left it virtually untouched. The nights could be chilly. I had to purchase a wool coat in addition to my texts. The traffic hub links up to all the best sectors. Great pneumatic tubes hover over the pathways like a static torus. They have the grandest hotels with terraced floors, each one overlapping the next. Other places are great silos of glass. The Central Business District is one of the oldest in Mother Africa. Anywhere you wish to worship, Nairobi is able to accommodate. There are mosques in the northern sector, and any corner of the city you shunt to has another cathedral, temple, or synagogue."

"Are the *matatus* as mad as Baba says?" she asked.

"Those infernal taxis? I'm sure," I replied. "I usually avoided them; the speed-rail service served my needs well enough. The only major drawback is that you have to ride in an upright coffin." I thought that was funny; but Jamai looked away.

"The East African Archive building is on Accra Road. All roads in that part of the city lead to it. It's home to the continental database we all rely on. The Archive is like a massive block, with slats of power-panels inset into its domed roof. Several hub tube lines connect to its roof deck. There are horseshoe arches around the street-level walls. The inlays between the arches are sprinkled with cotta paintings of Baba Kenyatta, Sister Jamaica, and even Benjamin Dlamini. Just past the lobby is a vast *eyvan*, an open vaulted hall reaching to the heights of the archive building. The public access terminals are housed in that area.

"The University lies in the upper northeast corner of the city, virtually next door to police headquarters. The Ngong Hills loom behind Delamere Avenue. At dawn they appear a spectral blue, like a holographic image that'll soon fade away. The eastward slopes overlook the Nairobi Historical Game Reserve. That's in the south of the city. It's silent now. Lions once roamed its grasses and giraffes seemed to tower over the glass offices our grandparents once sang about."

I collected our garbage with a sigh and tucked it in a waste chute behind Jamai's shoulder. "Nothing is left now except bugs and birds."

"And if I were to come, I might see them."

"No. As I said, they're all…"

"I heard you!" she snapped. "And I tell you I'd see them!" In one fluid movement she eased to her feet and crossed to the web-encrusted window. Her fingertips squeaked on the glass as she stroked it.

"Every night they sing for me, all the spirits shimmering in the night like heat rising off the plain. Simba pads to where I meditate, while antelope spronk among the tall grasses. All the enmity that once existed between predator and prey has passed. Sometimes, I even see people. Masai morani parade across the horizon and wave…"

The talk abruptly shifted onto an odd tangent. "They're not cultists," she said. "Sydelle's people are… non-dimensional, I suppose. They exist on a plane separate but parallel to ours, a dead zone of crushed atoms. Ngojama is similar, although I believe his race existed fully formed when he breached the veil between our planes. His exposure to our kind may have given him a measure of our moral inhibitions.

"Every 5,000 years, when our magnetic poles reverse, the barrier between our dimensions, renders it more… porous. Then a few more of Sydelle's lost people slip across to our sphere, and another few souls are lost."

"Maybe you could also explain why they keep calling you *Lepidopteran*. Even that freak Ngojama says it."

"It's a word from a dead language," she said listlessly. "It's the proper scientific term for the order of insects that includes butterflies and moths. I… I think it's meant as an insult. Please, can't we just stop talking?"

"You say this as though it were a lesson," I persisted. "Where did you learn this?"

"It was a lesson," she sighed. "I can't tell you where I learned it. I'll explain later, if we have one." I took a seat beside her. She refused the last nutrient bar I offered her. Together we sat huffing the humid air inside the shed; me hunched over my legs and she softly rapping the back of her skull on the wall with closed eyes.

"Rafiki, where is my grandmother?"

"Ummm…" Shit!

"Rafiki? What is it? Is she all right?"

This was not a good time. But she raised those pleading eyes, and all I could do was swallow. "Your uncle Kadar has placed her under house detention, pending a competency hearing. Once his experts have evaluated her…"

"What the hell for?"

I crouched in an awkward silence.

"It's because of me, isn't it? He wants to get anyone associated with me out of the way, even his own mother. He's trying to treat me like some kind of disease, and he's making my grandmother pay."

"Well, as long as we're getting everything out in the open…" Any competent therapist would probably say I was pushing for too much, that these details ought to be teased out of her one datum at a time. From my position, however, I wasn't expecting to live much past sunrise. "Kukuwazuka, what happened out there? How did you get here? You don't have to tell me, but I want to know. I want to help."

"I killed them, Rafiki. That's what happened."

A fist-sized lump rolled up and down her throat. Perspiration dripped from her forehead as she gazed down between her knees. Then she began her tale in a soft, toneless voice.

"Baba and I sat down to dinner just as we always did for the past eighteen years. I'd made his favorite curry, just as I always did. He set out the long-stemmed glasses he'd ordered from Paris for his and Mama's wedding night. Baba seemed downcast. He wouldn't even look at me. I didn't like him to be in these moods and asked what was the matter. He squeezed my hand and said nothing was wrong. Then we toasted the forthcoming girl's initiation, and mine.

"He asked me to refill his glass. I got as far as the pantry. I don't remember much beyond the dizziness and a little nausea. Then my knees sagged. Baba caught me, as if in a dream. The next thing I remember clearly was sitting up inside a bedroll deep in the rainforest.

"I didn't recognize the place in the dark. Camphor trees rose from the leaf mold. A pair of waterfalls poured through the flanks of a rocky outcrop, and an icy stream with no fish ran past the point where I'd slept. The land seemed wide open. The environment around Baba Elgonyi is stuffy with negative energy, but this place uplifted, as if the very electrons would buoy one up."

[*Her cinnamon complexion darkened as the story progressed. Perspiration beaded her skin in a fine sheen. She paused briefly, swaying with clenched teeth before she was able to continue.*]

"He must have drugged me…I think there was some paste on the bottom of my glass. I don't get queasy very often. That night it wouldn't let up. My wrist comp was no help. I tried using the EAC's geosynchronous sats to pinpoint my location. The wrist comp wouldn't respond, no matter how often or how frantically I tapped it. I couldn't waste time on that. So instead I watched the stars, the way Baba had always taught me on our camping expeditions, and let them guide my way.

"Twice more I tried booting up the comp. It only offered a bunch of stupid bleeps. I hiked over an uneven ridge, then climbed inside a hollow log to sleep off the nausea. I'd be better able to find my bearings in daylight anyhow. Luckily the trees were there to steady me, because when I crawled out of the log onto the mossy ground in the morning, the Sacred Mountain loomed over the landscape.

"In the darkness the trees had blocked my view, plus there were those drugs Baba had given me. In the daylight there was no hiding it. Sunshine sparkled off her snow-capped domes. Its sheer bulk blotted out most of the sky. I understood then why Baba had wrapped me in his parka. It had seemed nippy so close to the falls.

"Still, that was another clue. That put me below the Sipi River Falls, on Elgonyi's northwestern slope. Home would be on the opposite slope, due east. I could walk that in a matter of days.

"I don't know why I was so anxious to get home. I mean, wouldn't somebody be worried? Grandmother, S'manga… you? Some of my teachers were kind. Besides, where else could I go? Even if they didn't want me around, this was still my land, my home.

"I met Ngojama the second night. I wasn't expecting to see that thing again. I talked, though my skin curdled just being near him. He listened… he really listened. He probably could have taken me home, but he didn't offer. He sheltered me in the darkness of his den. Sweet Ngai, I didn't want to be there, not in the cold, or the enclosing walls. And oh, how he stank. But at least I wasn't alone.

"Sometime the following dawn he deposited me on the surface, and I continued east. The mountain had receded ten kilometers in the night. Ngojama must have been decent enough to speed me on my way while I slept. In three days time I'd made it to the outskirts of Kibarenge.

"I hadn't wanted to go there, either. Uncle Kadar had made it abundantly clear I wasn't welcome in his village. In any event, it was the closest place away from home, and I had to go someplace to make sense of my situation. I waited for nightfall and snuck to the public access kiosk outside their...

"What are they afraid of? Have you seen the stone wall surrounding Kibarenge? Did they partition parts off the Great Wall of China? The top of that monstrosity must have been three meters high. I couldn't have reached the top of it standing on tiptoes. Only the dome of their two mosques showed over the top of the wall.

"The kiosk's entry panel whisked on an inner track and admitted me inside. Even the public comm wouldn't log me in. I scanned my wrist comp, held it right up to the scanning lens. It kept insisting, over and over:

NO DATA PROCESSING POSSIBLE

TRY AGAIN HAVE A NICE DAY.

"I slumped down inside the kiosk, and for some reason the nausea returned. It hadn't occurred to me before there might be a more fundamental problem with my comp. These kiosks were supposedly infallible. The only thing that could have gone wrong would be if someone had attached an EMF scrambler to my comp lens while I was sedated four nights earlier. All my records were in there, Youssou. My identification, my medical history, school transcripts... everything that could tell anyone who I was... had been erased. The only ones who could have done it were Odu Molefe or Baba.

"My troubles hadn't even begun. I'd stepped out of the kiosk in a daze as bare feet padded along the western curve of the village wall. Around that curve appeared three women with spidery limbs, tall gangly things with bones jutting below their skin and their manes shorn close to their scalps.   They were like normal Poppy Girls, but... worse, blank. Soulless."

[*Soldier Poppys: I'd heard of such things, generally used as security at university labs or government ministries. Unlike most Poppy Girls, these bitches were programmed for aggressive, even brutal assaults on any party who trespassed against the ones commissioning them. This was the first instance I knew of where a Soldier Unit was specifically dispatched to cope with an individual. I had to wonder whether Molefe had put Kadar Dlamini up to this or if it was done on his own initiative.*]

"I didn't want to deal with them, so I stretched out my hand. Their long, body-length staffs easily sailed out of their grips and into mine. That's usually the end of things: people see what power I have and they back off. I… I only turned my back on them for a second to toss their weapons aside, and they piled into me."

[*Jamai's stomach roiled visibly as she swayed on the bench. A wave of sympathetic nausea swirled in my belly. Of all the terrible things our people had done to her, and knowing her uncle was behind it. I tried to reach out and steady her, to offer some comfort. She twitched her shoulder away from me, even though her glassy expression seemed to stare at nothing. She started to laugh, then touched the base of her skull.*]

"The first blow almost took my head off. One of them grabbed me from behind and pinned my arms to my sides. Another hitched her bony knuckles into my ribs. She was so… so tall her sweaty breasts pushed into my cheeks. The third one sprang onto the first girl's back and hooked her long legs around the second girl's hips. Then she leaned over the top of her sister's head and slid both her arms around my throat.

"The strangest part was how quiet our struggle was. They didn't say a word at first, only breathed in soft whispers while I wriggled and moaned. You're worried about the time I spend with snakes! I tell you, Rafiki, I'd never been mistreated the way those bitches did. My pulse throbbed against the crook of the third girl's arm as she cinched her elbow tighter.

"My arms had been twisted into the small of my back. While we swayed in the short grass, those three Poppy Girls began to chant. It was all in a monotone, a string of monosyllables… Die… die… die…"

"What…?"

She ignored me, or was too traumatized to acknowledge my presence. "People started coming around the walls to watch our dance. The girls notched themselves tighter around me. An ache began to grow, spiking through the top of my skull. The pain seemed to pound against my cheekbones. But I remember… the people took up the chant, even the little ones. 'Die,' they said. 'Die… die…' The only thing blocking out their stupid voices was the rasp of my own breath sandpapering up my windpipe. Then the third girl choked my air off completely.

"Damn them, it hurt. How could they just stand there? I'd never hurt them. They kept chanting, 'Die… die… die.' My skull pulsed over and a well of black nothingness swam in the periphery of my vision. It was shuttering in; everything was shrinking to a pinprick. I didn't have any more feeling in my fingers; they were like lumps.

"Sweet Ngai, even though everything was blurring, I could see *bibi* Cele. She was the only one not raising that awful chant. Holy father, it wasn't fair. She shouldn't have to see this. I didn't want to be there — I didn't want to die!"

Jamai became silent, rocking on her perch. Her knees were bunched into her chest while her face was swathed in her own hair. Rather stupidly my greatest worry was that her anguish would manifest as a surge of psychic energy and burst the walls, that every dog Child of Sydelle would rush to this shed post-haste. Despite these misgivings, the walls remained still. Again, I tried to comfort her, but her arms flailed at me. After that she seemed to coil tighter into a fetal ball.

"The next thing I remember," she said, now in a wheeze, "I was on my knees rasping in the dirt. Not even the night birds sang. But I could breathe again. I ached all over, but I was alive.

I didn't know who called off the girls except… my body was drenched in some faintly metallic-smelling goo, and a series of hair-thin sticky strips.

"A livid ache pulsed around my eyelids. Still, I was getting my vision back. From what I could tell, the people were drawing back. Only Cele was still close by, both hands stuffed in her mouth. I'd only just begun to notice the white bones scattered in a narrow radius around my knees."

Her voice croaked. "Sweet Ngai, forgive me. Nobody called the Poppy Girls off. I… I panicked. They were going to kill me. Baba, I'm sorry, I just wanted them to get off me. I didn't think. Well, the… the Elders barked orders.

"Nobody wanted to rush out there and detain me, but the Elders, egged on by Uncle Kadar, badgered the young men with their ceremonial staffs. Grandmother threw herself into the thick of the melee, shouting for me to run. They were trying not to rough her up — she was 99 years old after all — but they managed to shuffle her to one side. So, I ran. I left her, and I ran…"

The awkward silence was unmercifully brief this time. "You son of a bitch."

My head jerked up. "I beg your…"

"You son of a bitch! Why did you make me remember that? I thought you were my friend. How could you do this to me?"

My mouth dropped. "To you? *To you*? You're questioning me, after everything I've done? I busted my ass trying to help you. They sent me to prison on account of… oh my god, you ungrateful bitch! You're more trouble than you're worth sometimes, you know that?"

We all say stupid things when we're young; but nobody could've said anything as brainless as what I'd just blurted. I regretted it immediately, but it was already out there. Without a word, Jamai spun and stomped toward the door of the hutch, ignoring my protestations. The door banged shut, rattling the entire structure with the force of her anger.

I lunged for it, but the handle didn't budge. It wouldn't even yield to my kicking. With her mind this focused on keeping it shut, the door remained as solid as ebony. And my foot was a throbbing mess.

From the window, I spied her stamping through the grass directly outside the workman's hutch. I feared she'd blunder past the icons I'd posted for our protection. Some instinct caused her to swing back and scream, "*Nini? Kwa nini?*" A mountainous shadow with a bristling coif waited beyond the circle of trees shading the hutch.

It stretched a paw with a single curved claw in its palm, but it didn't stray into our safety zone. Those markers I'd burned into the tree bark still held their ancient terrors for it. Jamai stood ramrod straight, fingers to her lips. The creature beckoned, and she actually advanced a step toward him.

She raised her right calf, left it dangling while a huff steamed whitely from the beast's flattened muzzle. Jamai eased her leg back to the dirt. Her hands clutched at her skull as she gave it a vigorous shake. Our visitor smacked its upraised paw into the ground. I exhaled gratefully as Ngojama pressed its arms down. With its mane sliding after it, the latest freak burrowed into the earth for the night.

The next target for her anger was her "mother". It regarded her from a pile of hoops coiled around an abandoned geothermal drill-head. A slick heavy tarp had been wrapped around the broken drill and Jamai's pet — mother, I'm not sure anymore — was cozied around the three meters of shaft still protruding from the ground.

Jamai's hands flailed at the snake, shrieking heaven knows what; her high- pitched babbling plus the distance blurred her words. On at least two occasions she jabbed a finger toward the tinted glass where I stared out. The snake endured this abuse with more equanimity than I could have managed. Still, even I was surprised by the stealth with which it ambushed her. While she was ranting, a heavy cable as thick around as her thigh settled around her waist.

She gazed down, suddenly silent and a little uncertain, as a second loop spun around her, clutching her from hips to breasts. Both her hands held it close while she pedaled in the oily hoops curling around her calves. With a gentle tug, the snake pulled Jamai over to one side. With infinite leisure, it rolled her around to a seated position with her back pressed to the drill shaft.

One hand rubbed at her brow while the other still held the coil around her middle like a lifeline. Her lips moved, mouthing silent denials. The tip of the snake's tail curled up and brushed an unruly strand from her cheek. After a while of this quiet communion, Jamai's legs slid to the ground. Her chin craned upward, exposing her throat to the moonlight. Her "mother" accepted the invitation, enfolding her neck in a massive coil.

I tried the door again, but the handle might as well have been welded into place. An explosive charge only battered my shoulder. There was nothing for it now. All I could do was to ease down as close to the window as possible and keep watch.

And hope that tonight would be like all the other nights she'd come to this end.

Day Three: Love, Loss and Awkward Shelters

WERE THOSE DRUMS BEATING INSIDE MY HEAD? No, I hadn't had a drink since that night in Nairobi, before… never mind. I creaked to a semi-erect position, using the wall as a backscratcher. The dawn light slanting through the windows highlighted the airborne dust motes.

I wiped at the cool film of condensation on the glass. A trio of shorthaired, scantily clad girls approached from the east, each tapping meter-long tom-toms that dangled from straps slung over their shoulders. Behind them followed more of those ape-men I'd eluded the day before, a half-dozen of them this time. Bringing up the rear was Bren Auflauring.

I bolted outside, not caring that the door clattered against the hutch's outer walls loud enough to be heard for miles. Five hundred meters were all that separated our compound from Auflauring's troop.

Jamai was still bundled from the neck down in a reptilian corset. Her upper lip protruded from her mother's coils, which breathed in tandem with her. One of these days I should whip this security-blanket issue out of her. I was too obliging as things stood, but I usually couldn't deny her the serenity this experience seemed to grant.

Oh well. Serenity would have to wait. "Psst," I said. "Jamai, wake up."

She didn't stir in her serpent cocoon. I tried calling again, louder, with as little effect. Maybe it was a sign of how deranged I had become. I glared at the snake. "Oi, you. Wake her ass up."

I turned to the figures approaching in the mists, almost at the gates of the station. A sharp c-r-a-c-k and a muffled yelp tore out behind me. Jamai blinked, then began to push onto her knees as the snake oozed off her. She stood on wobbly legs, rubbing the welt rising on her behind.

I managed a feeble smile. "We have company," I told her with false cheer.

Auflauring and his ape-men crossed into the substation's perimeter, preceded by his blank-faced girls, none of whom appeared to be out of their school years. Auflauring raised one hand and his followers waited as he strode ahead. He seemed too preoccupied to be certain they'd obeyed his unspoken command, though in fact they'd done so. His fists remained balled knuckle-white at his side.

"*Der junge,*" he said in a clipped guttural tone, "you are not a part of these proceedings."

"I wouldn't be anywhere else," I replied.

"Very well." Slowly he glided back into the ranks of his acolytes. His right arm snapped up, and with a flick of his wrist, the three serving wenches dashed on pitter-patter feet from the rear. Once they'd circled around to the front, they reformed into a sort of giddy picket line, padding straight for us. Except that now they didn't appear as harmless as they had from a distance. Each girl cradled to her low-cut bosom a twin-barreled prod with fist-sized power packs tucked into their armpits.

"Kill the boy," Auflauring said. "Bring us the Lepidopteran."

Taking my elbow in hand, Jamai tipped her chin to face the sun. Then she snapped her head down and stared full-on at the approaching party.

Perhaps it was on account of the many boreholes punched into the grounds; possibly the soil had already been loosened on the same account. Perhaps Jamai was simply tired of being harassed by these wuolos. But at fifty paces, with a united squeal, every girl plunged up to the hips into the hard-packed ground.

Their prods became even less of an issue once the weapons breezed past us. They clattered into the maintenance shed, and the door slammed closed on the lot of them. Well, except for the prod that Jamai's thoughts had plunked into my hands.

The girls struggled and panted, only succeeding in settling themselves up to their chests. The crimson soil rippled with a kind of tinkling crunch as the ground solidified around its prisoners, their arms now pinioned in the embracing Earth.

Jamai's fingers brushed through the girls' scalps as she passed between them. Auflauring retreated, first behind his ape-men and then outside the compound itself. The girls gazed blankly up at her, a question seemingly on their lips. I skirted through them without a word.

"What did you do to them?" Jamai asked.

"It was a necessary procedure," Auflauring shrugged. "It is possible to feed *unsere die Lehrerin*, that is, our Mistress Sydelle, a portion of their life force. The collector is calibrated to target the psychological wavelength which we believe is situated in the human cerebellum."

Jamai seemed to understand that balderdash. "You fed her their minds."

"Only the consciousness," Auflauring said. "Mind, soul, it all comes to the same thing. We've found they're much better off after the procedure. It's much less invasive than a lobotomy, wouldn't you agree?"

The morning was still cool, but perspiration had already started on Jamai's brow. She was leaning her face into the back of her palm. "Nobody dies, *fraulein*," he insisted. "Besides… they do make useful servants."

"What's the matter with you people?" Jamai was shaking her head. Her voice began with soft pleading, but it rose in velocity and pitch. "Why do so many people have to be hurt for your mistress? Why do so many have to die? What in the hell do you want with me?"

"Alas, fraulein, I cannot agree with your assessments," Auflauring said. "I truly don't see there is anything the matter with us. As for your final query, on that score I may be able to enlighten you. Sydelle also had her moment of doubt. In spite of her youth, she was a frail child, weak in body as well as mind, as her subsequent mutation readily attests."

"Her what? What is he babbling?" Jamai silenced my questions with a shake of the head.

Auflauring wagged his finger at her, not with any malicious intent, but simply in the spirit of a schoolmaster summoning his favorite pupil to the front of the class. "Your form, however, is a superb vessel, more than able to contain our Lehrerin's essence. If your Dr. Nlebela's assumptions are correct, your hormonal adaptations may offer some protection from any possible mutagenic effects."

"May?" I barely contained my laughter. "You expect her to take this Sydelle's place? You don't expect her to agree to this operation?"

"As I said, Herr Hadebe, this does not concern you."

"I'll be the judge of that… nor have we come to negotiate," he added.

"You can't do it," Jamai said.

"On the contrary…" Auflauring began, but she cut him off with a vicious laugh. In fact, she fell over her knees with giggles.

"I mean, you literally can't," she finally spluttered. "You don't have Sydelle's mortal remains. Hell, you fisis don't even know where Elias' disciples interred her."

"Only half true, fraulein," Auflauring said. "While her remains are not at hand, I believe the Collector operates both ways. If a chosen victim's essence can be directed to sustain the Lehrerin, it should be equally possible for her essence to be downloaded into the chosen vessel, provided she is in the act of absorbing said vessel's consciousness, naturally. And the Collector is on hand to act as a sort of grounding force."

"Did any of that make sense to you?" I whispered to Jamai.

"I'm afraid so." She said, then shouted back at him, without a great deal of conviction, "I won't be a party to this!"

"That choice is no longer yours." Auflauring's henchmen also had weapons, which they trained on us. These were conventional shrapers, fashioned with a meter-long barrel ending in a cushioned stock. A buffer panel with flared wings like an ax-head was placed between stock and barrel; an ammo tin rested flat-side down where buffer and barrel joined.

I take pains to describe this because these things are such vicious bastards. The shraper pellets are designed to shatter a few meters from the target. Instead of one shell penetrating your body, you may have dozens, each a serrated-edged terror flying at a minimum of 200 km. an hour. You don't have to be accurate to use one; anyone within this weapons' proximity could be flayed alive.

"I thought they needed you whole," I said. But she was trying hard to shove me behind her.

"Her figure is more than capable of sustaining a few minor wounds," Auflauring shrugged. "You, on the other hand… well, I did warn you."

"Stay behind me," she said.

"Wait a minute, you can't…"

"Shut up and get behind me!" With a violent shove, she sent me tumbling head over buttocks. As she flung up her arms, the shrapers puffed.

For a quarter-second the pellets were silent as they streaked across the savannah. As they neared us a piercing shriek rose in pitch. At thirty meters, each pellet cracked in a blue puff with a noise like dry corn popping. A barrage, like repeated strokes of thunder, deafened us as a hail of streaking embers bore down. At ten meters, they stopped.

They just stopped. Each piece thumped into some kind of barrier before dropping onto the grass. The barrage pummeled at us like a cloud of locusts, but could not penetrate the psychic barrier that Jamai had thrown up. Auflauring jabbed at us screaming, "*Schnell, schnell!*" His apes closed ranks, forming a semi-circle that did them no good whatsoever.

Once Jamai peeked through her crossed arms, then screwed up her face in redoubled concentration. "How are you doing this?" I shouted.

"I don't know!" she screamed back.

"Well throw it back at them!"

"I can't. I'll kill them!"

She couldn't keep up this mental barrier forever either. Those shrapers' ammo tins carried upwards of 300 pellets. All it would take is one slip of concentration and we'd be done. Well, I'd be done; she'd only be captured. "Kukuwazuka, I have an idea! Listen, you're drawing power from the local biosphere…"

"Yes! So what!"

"So can't you pick out individual targets?" My finger pointed there, there and there, at each one of Auflauring's apes.

She shook her head violently. "I… I can't! I don't want to kill them!"

"You won't have to! Trust me! This'll work!"

The rich cocoa-butter scent of her perspiration mingled with my coarse reek. My throat seemed full of cotton as she slowly lowered her arms and spread them wide. When her chin arched back, the first two men at either end of the firing line peeled off to one side.

The wind picked up, blowing a hot smothering gunpowder stench back in our enemies' eyeballs. Still, I doubt it was on that account that their eyes rolled into their hairless skulls. The shrapers slipped from their grips. The remaining two fellows crumbled to their knees, but they fought manfully to keep up the firing.

Auflauring's stare whipped toward each man as they flopped like trees onto their bare backs. Which pretty much left him isolated and vulnerable.

It took him a grand total of four seconds to comprehend these facts, adequate time for his face to become paler still. His hand began a slow descent into the left hip pocket of his robe. That was as abruptly snatched away as a crystalline gem ripped through the fabric. It streaked past Jamai's cheek. The trapped girls ducked their heads as the gem homed in on a nearby tree and vanished in a poof of crystalline dust.

Auflauring had maintained a dignified demeanor throughout this encounter, and I had to admire how well he kept on in that spirit. Jamai exhaled, her waist-length curls billowing on a psychic wind. She rotated her neck with a sharp pop. Auflauring retreated one step; then, with an "oof!" his body dropped out of sight.

Only after he disappeared did Jamai sag, bracing her palms on her knees as an explosive breath huffed from her chest. Her hair abruptly flattened over her neck, and her entire body seemed to be racked with shivers. She nodded yes to my anxious demands, she was all right. She clutched at her right arm as we crossed the field.

We found Auflauring in the same predicament as his young ladies, in his case, up to his neck. His granite face burned red; he must have been having difficulty breathing, owing to the pressure of the Earth surrounding him. Even so, he was able to gaze up at Jamai and remark, "You don't look well."

She ducked her head and managed a giggle.

"Jamai, this Euro wuolo tried to kill us," I said.

"Don't be silly, he was only trying to kill you."

"How flattering," I grumbled.

She braced herself on her knees in front of Auflauring. "I'm not going to hurt you," she told him, wetting her lips. "But I need to know how to free Ngojama."

He snorted, "That intransigent *schwein*? He was charged with delivering you into our care, not in assisting your liberty."

"Apparently, you didn't see their little tiff the other night," I muttered. They both glared at me from the corners of their eyes.

"I already smashed your crystal ball," she said. "How can you still be controlling him?"

"Pff! That was an external control device, a glorified remote. The true power of our Lehrerin is manifested in the tattoo branded in his shoulder. It acts as a psychic transponder, if you will."

"How can you be so cold? He's a living thing, a lost child of Ngai."

"Like yourself." Auflauring's sweaty brows knitted together. "Kindred spirits, the two of you. *Ja, ja*, I see. Adrift in an unfeeling world. We could help you with that," he grinned.

"How do I free Ngojama?" she insisted.

"Why would you want to? This is no fluttering insect. He is a *menschenfeind* from ancient times, steeped in the blood of his victims. Why do you think we recruited him? He is not likely to thank you for the service you're proposing."

"I don't care!" She rocked on her heels, adapting a placating smile. "It'd give me emotional comfort."

Auflauring closed his eyes and wheezed. "You will have to remove the brand."

"Fine."

"*Nein*, fraulein, you will have to remove it surgically. It is embedded three centimeters into his epidermis. You will have to cut into that much skin and carve beneath the surrounding tissue."

I thought her cheeks might have turned a new tinge of green. But she nodded, and actually thanked the bastard. She left him with a kiss on top of his bald pate, then rose and brushed herself off as she walked away.

I followed close behind. "Wait, you're just going to leave him?"

"Why not? He's harmless where he is. Call your father if it worries you, he can… dig." Her footsteps slowed as a glazed stare shadowed her features. "Oh no!"

"What is it?"

"Ngojama!"

We'd put forty meters behind us. She pelted back to Auflauring. By the time she was within twenty meters, she was flapping her arms and screaming, "No, no!" Auflauring's stare was directed at the ground churning around his throat. There was hardly time for a last gulp of air as the earth surged over the top of his head.

Jamai's momentum was arrested by a forward lunge. Her knees rasped bloodily into the dirt an arm's length from where Auflauring had been. The shraper I cradled was useless; how was I supposed to shoot at something I couldn't see?

If I seemed frantic, Jamai's situation was problematically worse. Her mouth yawned wide and a strangled gag gurgled in the back of her throat. I tried shaking her out of her trance, but her eyes bulged rounder by the moment. If anything, the rasping only worsened.

Auflauring's head popped back to the surface. Jamai's breath wheezed sharply back into her lungs as her hand shot to her mouth. She fumbled to her feet, staggering drunkenly to the drill-head where she and her mother had spent the night.

There could be no blaming her. A closer examination showed that only Auflauring's head had been returned to us. His eyes were still locked in a disbelieving stare.

"There's a nice lot lying here that you might want to collect," I coughed into our portable comm unit. The rusty soil had settled, though the wind still stirred a few stray particles. "Jomoro can home in on this signal."

"Are you well?" Father's voice sang clearly in my earpiece, despite the kilometers between us. I'd given him a basic outline of everything that'd transpired thus far, including the appearance of Auflauring. "Did they injure either of you?"

Jamai's had sat with her back toward me atop a massive coiled shaft since Auflauring's head had been returned to us. I couldn't touch the thing. I just left it; it wasn't going anywhere. As deeply as she breathed, it never seemed to be breath enough.

"We're not hurt," I reported.

The bodies of Auflauring's apes fanned around us in a 180-degree arc. The girls were no closer to freeing their shoulders of the embracing Earth, and regarded their predicament with a good amount of childish puzzlement.

"Bring the earth moving mahutis," I added to Father. "We've got a few souls stuck in the ground."

He probably didn't understand the gist of that remark, as he only murmured a flat "Uh-hmm. What about Auflauring? Jomoro is very interested in questioning him about this affair. Where is he?"

"He's… he's dead, Father."

I logged off before he could interrogate me any further. I was only too painfully aware of how badly this would reflect on Jamai, on top of that incident with the Soldier Poppy Girls. I jammed a signal prod into the ground outside the geothermal substation. The prod began to strobe red. The authorities could find the bodies without our help now.

Butterflies clustered thickly around Jamai's torso like a living blanket. They peeled away in a riotous fan of colors as I stepped toward her. "He wasn't expecting to die," she said. Her skin was still icy with perspiration. "I lived it with him… he couldn't even scream… I could taste the dirt filling his mouth…"

"If we could explain the circumstances, Jomoro might…"

"Explain what? Some brute out of mythology sucked him into the ground after I put him there? Do you expect a judge won't laugh the three of us out of court?"

"He saw it… he saw you defending us!"

"And who's going to corroborate his story? Which of our learned Elders will leap to my defense?" Her gaze dropped, staring blankly across the field at the girls who'd grown quiescent in their earthen wombs. Several butterflies took an interest in them as well. "Rafiki, can you imagine Jomoro trying to lay such a report before the Ministry of Justice?"

That thought didn't require any examination at all. "No."

"How long do we have?"

"An hour, two at best."

She nodded and pushed herself off the fragment of shaft. "It'll have to be enough. I'm going to trust you with something," she said, "something I may not have a right to offer. First, there is one thing more I have to do."

"Cele Dlamini," I ventured.

"Uncle Kadar has wrongly accused her on my behalf. I have to go to her. Today. I owe her this much."

There are times when we're of one mind on a given subject. Fortunately, the Children of Sydelle had left us with a large selection of hovers from which to choose.

FROM A DISTANCE, KIBARENGE DIDN'T APPEAR MUCH DIFFERENT from Baba Elgonyi. From what one could see of the village at all through the narrow gates in their defensive wall, at any rate. Jamai hadn't said the half of it; that turgid mass encompassed Kibarenge like folds of glistening clay awaiting firing in a potter's oven. Certainly their fields were more lush, and the minarets of two mosques spired at each corner of the walls.

The Soldier Poppys also showed a noticeable difference. Perhaps these were a reserve unit awaiting deployment at Kadar Dlamini's discretion. Their bare feet scarcely scuffed the grass as they padded in our direction. Jamai jerked to a halt and shuddered, her lower lip between her teeth. I stepped around her, drew out a whistle I'd appropriated from our stolen hover, and put it to my lips. One shrill blast brought the genetic imbeciles to a swift and sudden stop.

The three stood at attention, their brown skin glistening without the smallest bead of perspiration. Holy Ngai, she was right. These brutes were Amazons. They'd put an Olympic-class power lifter to shame. Fortunately, they were also conditioned to obey commands. With luck, perhaps any command.

I stepped forward, twirling the whistle on its cord. "Well done!" I called, deepening my voice to mimic an Elder's best orations. "You have fulfilled your obligations and captured the renegade." I ignored Jamai's arched stare and continued. "Now return to the Council and bring forth Kadar Dlamini, that he may view the prize."

The Amazons curtsied, three in a row, then loped single file back into Kibarenge. Jamai nudged me, "Well done, fisi," she said, slapping my shoulder. She shuddered as our would-be killers retreated. "Now we'll see if Uncle swallows the bait."

Small worry. Flies can never resist the smell of carrion. Before many more minutes passed, Kadar Dlamini shuffled through the dry stalks of sorghum. He'd about come level with a pocked kopje split through the middle by a rising seedling when he spied Jamai striding around me to meet him. The Soldier Poppys dogging his tracks bumped into his rear once he abruptly stopped. The other village Elders wisely stayed right where they were, near the containment wall.

His staff hung on the tips of his fingers as Jamai crossed her arms and waited for him. He recovered enough sense to put two fingers to his lips, probably to call on his escorts for assistance. Jamai cut him off before he blew the first whistle. "Unless you want a repeat of what happened on my last visit, you'll tell those soulless husks to be somewhere else."

Kadar's staff cantered in his loose grasp. He wiped his free palm, surely as wet, across his dappled brow, then swept his staff thirty degrees upward. The soldiers jogged back inside the gates of Kibarenge. To all appearances, Kadar stalked mercilessly forward. "You would dare to come back here… in those garments… after what you…"

"Shut up, dunglips."

There's a surprise. I never expected Kukuwazuka to openly show such disrespect to an Elder, let alone one who was a paramount leader in her own family. His voice rose an octave. "How dare… I am a Chief among these Elders."

"Then shut up, Chief Dunglips."

Another Elder bellowed with good spirits before noticing he stood alone in his amusement. Jamai advanced toward her uncle, who idled backwards in time with her advance. "I'm not going to bandy words with you," she said. "I've come to demand Cele Dlamini's release."

"My mother is unwell," he intoned unsteadily. "She suffers from your influence. Once she has been deprogrammed, it is in the province of our kiama to re-assess her mental status."

"Yesss! Like Odu Molefe did in choosing a master in the Children of Sydelle to assess mine," Jamai nodded. "Have you always bore such a level of disrespect for your mother? She will be released. Unconditionally. Now!"

"Supposing I refuse? Will you murder me as well?" Kadar squeaked.

A humorless smile curved Jamai's lips. "Nothing so final. If my grandmother is not freed within the next five minutes, I'm going to do something that will bring extreme discomfort to your household. I'm going to move in with you."

Kadar's eyes did a remarkable distention. "Th… th… that's not permissible."

"You can't prevent it. Do as I say, or I'll collect my belongings straightaway and set up house. I'm young and impatient. Don't take too long debating your options."

He set a new distance record in hurrying back to his fellow Elders. They ducked their heads low, glaring in Jamai's direction. As one body, they retreated to Kibarenge. Two minutes later, a frail old woman strode proudly to greet her granddaughter.

There could be no greater contrast between the two of them. This was the woman who practically raised Jamai during her father's frequent absences. Jamai and Cele Dlamini wandered the grasses outside Kibarenge, oblivious of the staring eyes along the outskirts of the village. Far from looking up to her, at least on the physical level, Jamai towered half a meter over the venerable old woman, and still she kept her chin tucked in deference to her.

I couldn't hear a word of what passed between them, and I wouldn't ask if nothing was volunteered. I glanced occasionally at the time readout on my wrist comm, while keeping one eye tuned to the horizon. They shared a last, lingering embrace. Then Jamai strode purposefully back to my side.

"Grandmother will be contacting her friends in Old Nairobi," she said, *sotto voce*. "She's sure they'd be willing to take her in, on a communal basis." She gazed over her shoulder to where her grandmother stood, alone on the plain. "I don't like leaving her alone like that. Do you think I should stay, just to make certain…?"

"Kukuwazuka," I insisted, "Jomoro is bound to have found Auflauring's body by now."

She nodded, breezing past me to the pilot's hatch on the skiff. "I need your promise," she said, "never to tell anyone about what you're about to see. I've made a pledge to someone dear to me, and I must ask that you honor it."

"For Christ's sake, Kukuwazuka, after all the times we've…"

"Rafiki, please!"

I wet my lips, still a bit leery. "Is this something I'll regret later, or that'll endanger you?"

"The only creature who'll be in danger," she said, "is the one I'm going to introduce you to. He can offer us shelter from the Children of Sydelle and Ngojama."

I gave her a provisional nod. She inclined her head in turn and waved me into the passenger's seat.

Jamai took the stick of our purloined skiff as we left Kibarenge. It had made good sense to switch vehicles; the authorities would find it difficult to trace us without our acquisition's GPS signature, assuming it even had one. We proceeded due east for a half hour. Eventually we caught sight of, two kilometers distant, the jade dome of Baba Elgonyi's mosque, a small pock on the vast horizon. Jamai made a long sweeping arc around the nearby shambas of our designated tillers. Perhaps she remembered the times as young *totos* we plucked weeds and led our father's mahutis in laying soil restoratives.

Her lips trembled. I suppose my heart also beat quicker. If Jomoro had any lookouts posted, they'd surely have spotted us. Luckily we were able to plunge into the forest without drawing pursuit.

Intermittent patches of daylight occasionally penetrated the gloom of the forest canopy. Still, Jamai's presence in the skiff in no way diminished the respect that flora accorded her. Vines continued to scrape along the pods. But for the most part, bushes and saplings tipped at a thirty-degree angle to let us pass.

Eventually she brought the skiff to a grinding halt in an open area where the sun cast slanting shafts onto a massive mound swathed in tangled vines. The high-pitched whine of the skiff's propulsion pods surrendered to a subtler hum, a mixture of several species of bee unseen in the enclosing foliage. Wings beat through the trees, fading away as their owners fled our unsightly arrival.

I must have wondered aloud what she found so damned fascinating about this place. It was a glade, nothing more. She leaned over the side, and her arm traced an arc over the mulch-covered ground. Leaves fluttered on a psychically driven breeze, scattering in all directions away from... a flight of steps?

The vines tendered down in an impenetrable curtain over an ebony portal that appeared refreshingly new. "Our fathers say that Benjamin Dlamini came to us as a man out of the wilderness. Before he came, he had no past, gave no one his history," Jamai said quietly. "Have you ever wondered what part of the wilderness he wandered from?"

She vaulted catlike from her seat, then leaned over the pilot's seat to stroke my face. "I want to show you some answers."

She skipped up the steps, dragging me behind. Only once did she pause to draw breath. Then she stared up the heights of the vine curtain and called, "Grandfather, I've come home! And I bring a good friend!"

From inside a voice echoed, "Come in, *toto*, and be welcome!"

Jamai breezed through the entry. I was still gawking at that vegetable wall when her hand flashed out of the darkness and clawed at my shirt. With a short sharp tug, she jerked me inside.

"Watch for the sinkhole by the carpet," she said, pointing two meters ahead. "I haven't got around to fixing it."

A musty stench wafted from the floor mats, but that was at least tolerable next to the pungent disinfectant scent that permeated the walls and tiles. Something rattled insistently in a ceramic bowl above and to our right. Jamai whispered, "*Samahani, nurudogo,*" and padded to the wall.

She stood on her toes and reached up, rattling the *nurudogo*, a translucent ball that gave off a steady light, in her palm. She tossed the ball to the floor, which bounced back to her palm emitting a golden glow as bright as the midmorning sun. This ball she pitched to the ceiling, where it adhered and flattened.

The new light did little to improve the architecture that consisted primarily of long winding hallways with doors every few meters. The carpet was rotted to tatters, and a gaping hole yawned just inside the vine-covered entry.

I hasten to mention the recent addition of ill-fitting panels, pressed unevenly to the moldering walls with an overabundance of carpenter's adhesive, and the cracked holes where the staples were laid, apparently at point blank range. It was a restoration job of an incompetence rivaled only by government contract work, and I said so out loud.

Unfortunately, Jamai was standing beside me. Her bright expression crumbled as she ducked her head. I apologized too late for my stupidity.

"Young men never change." The deep voice jerked me upright. A cloak fluttered up the right-hand corridor. Two lights probed brightly from beneath its hood, which crinkled toward Jamai. "Always shooting their mouths off. Are you sure you brought the right friend?"

"I am, Grandfather," she said, glancing uncomfortably my way. "Rafiki, this is the man who's given me shelter these last few weeks." She took my hand and lifted it toward two decaying gloves extending from the sleeves of the cloak.

"Youssou, this is Esaias Pahoran Dlamini, father of our founding father, Benjamin Dlamini."

"He's what… oww!" The small hairs rising on my arms should have been a clue to what was coming. Sparks fizzled through my bones as our fingers touched. I yanked myself back. "That's impossible. Benjamin Dlamini died centuries ago. And what the devil was that?"

"A momentary static charge. My substance presently consists of highly charged particles. Sorry," he said, not without a chuckle. "Really, you had that coming."

"Grandfather!" Jamai took his arm, which billowed like a balloon where she gripped it. They meandered several meters along the winding corridor. It wasn't so far that I couldn't overhear their conversation. "Have you found…?"

"Not yet, *toto*. Have faith."

"Grandfather, I… I have nothing left. I have so much to talk about."

The hood bobbed several times. "We can talk later. Go to the rectory, meditate for as long as you need. I'll take care of him."

My chin snapped up. "You'll what?"

She swiveled her tear-stained cheeks in my direction. "I need some time alone, Rafiki. Grandfather will show you around." The aforementioned specter floated my way.

"Kukuwazuka? Where are you going? Where will you be?" I shouted.

"Close by."

"For how long?"

"I don't know!" Flinging up her arms, she bolted into the darkness of the hall to our left. Her grandfather and I faced each other from opposite ends of the chamber.

"Well," I said.

"Well," he agreed.

After a moment, he inquired, "By any chance did you bring her a change of outfits?"

"It wasn't my first priority. No."

We had nothing more to say for a while. The hem of his robe shifted as though a leg was twitching under there. I wriggled my fingers. Finally we both harrumphed. "There are refreshments two doors down, to the left," he said. "She brought juice and water to boil for tea or espresso."

"Asante, no. I prefer coffee. Black." He found that amusing. "I suppose you know what she's been accused of."

"I am. She acted in her own defense."

"Yes, yes. Actually, I don't know. I've no idea what to believe."

"And yet you are here."

"I don't abandon my friends."

"Young man, I'd like to try something," he said, crossing the chamber.

Oh great, I thought. *Is that a code phrase they always use before rooting about in your skull?*

"May I?" He offered a hand, palm up.

I heaved my shoulders heavily. He was polite about it, at least. His glove hovered eight centimeters from my brow. In spite of the icy tendrils pushing into my brains, I held my ground. The probe lasted no more than a moment, but it seemed to have told him a great deal. He fell back two steps with his hood bowed. One hand stroked his spectral chin.

"Interesting," he said. "Does my granddaughter know?"

"No," I admitted. "Are you going to tell?"

"No, I should leave that to you. What are your intentions toward my granddaughter?"

"That's a bit of a personal question, don't you think?"

"I am her grandfather."

"I don't know that! I don't know anything about you, other than the fact that you're... you're...bloody hell!" I swore and stormed down the indicated corridor for a drink. With any luck, he might have a beer around.

He was still haunting the inner chamber when I returned. All she had stocked in her portable cooler was a six-pack of tomato extract. He picked up precisely where we'd left off.

"Fair enough," he agreed. "What did the two of you do together as children?"

"We picked bugs out of our father's gardens, chased birds away at the springs. She tried to involve me with her snakes, but I prefer fur and feathers."

"Aha. That bothers you, does it?"

"Of course it does! Don't you find it a little...?"

"What? Unorthodox? Obscene? Worrisome, to be sure. She's explained that habit, otherwise I would never allow it. Even so, were it not for the benign presence hovering close by..."

I stopped. "What benign presence? I've never seen..."

"Not surprising. Living eyes can never see the departed."

"Don't patronize me, you... you walking electric socket."

The bulbs inside his hood shifted from pale blue to flaming crimson. "Try this, then, whelp. The mind — or soul if it pleases you — is energy with positive as well as negative poles. Naturally, the spirit can never truly be destroyed. When did you discover Jamai's erratic habit?"

"The whole village found out when she tumbled out of a tree on a python's tail," I said, grinning at the memory. "She and my sister Ahela were listening to a traveling storyteller from the branches above him, and she slipped. Sometime later we went on an outing to the slopes of Mt. Elgon. It was an enlightening trip."

"Umm-hmm."

"We did not have sex!"

"Of course," the specter replied innocently. "You do realize those beasts are acting against their own natures when they cuddle her? We can only hope she'll grow out of this stage and find a little, shall we say, human companionship."

"This benign presence… is this the same one she asked you to search for?"

His cowl stiffened into a triangular point. "How did you know?"

Suspicion confirmed, I nodded. "That's what she called her snake on our outing. As long as we're on the subject, what's to keep that blue maniac from barging into this wreckage?"

"Ngojama?" Our host's hands formed an inverted bowl between us as we walked. "Not possible," he said. "The foundation stones are impregnated with special wards at each compass point of this temple. They form a sort of psychically energized umbrella field to repel evil influences. Only the pure of heart can abide here."

My stomach gurgled. "Then why haven't I withered up and died?" *Did that wraith just sigh?*

"It's not intended to repel persons of average character. Your nature is impatience, a common trait of youth. Therefore, you were allowed to pass. Oh, you may experience some minor discomfort, nausea… dear me, green on brown, that is a sickly complexion.

"My predecessor," he continued, "God rest his soul, had a devil of a time persuading our Tanzanian contractor to insert those baubles into the foundations. Fortunately certain of our members happened to be persons of means."

I grinned. "You bribed them."

His hood slumped into great wrinkled folds. "Yesss! May I continue? The crystals were formed of the purest elements, dating to when the Earth first cooled. Elias chose this site well; it lies at the intersection of several leys. When the planet's energy fields course through these leys, they can form a potent refractionary field."

"You're trying to confuse me."

"And how easily it is done," the spirit murmured. "Would it be simpler to say the wards act as a mirror repelling negative impulses? As I said, the mind has opposite poles, though these are based on emotional rather than EMF factors. Jealousy versus loving kindness, patience versus hastiness, love versus hate."

His hands came apart and trembled, as though some force were pressing them apart. "These influences would be refracted by the crystal matrixes. This in turn stimulates an electromagnetic pulse that is directed back at the source." Sparks burst from his hands as they connected.

"And how do these crystals or wards…"

"The wards are crystalline in nature."

"Yes, if you say so. How could they determine what's evil and what's not?"

"By the negative actions of the invader toward its fellow beings."

An ache began to pulse through my temples. "You're talking in circles. Have you been studying quantum mechanics?"

"Don't be ludicrous."

"Even assuming any of this is true, and personally I think it's a load of hogwash, why should I believe you? Electromagnetism is one of the weakest physical forces imaginable."

"Naturally, in its unfocused state it would be. Our crystal wards are able to concentrate that energy, just as Sydelle's minions abuse their potential by murdering the innocent."

"Yes, I noticed. Jamai's getting pretty adept at smashing those things."

"They're crystal. Of course they're fragile."

"One thing still bothers me," I admitted. "Why do those bastards keep the bodies of their victims? Why not simply dispose of them?"

"I don't know. I've never understood that aspect. They've collected bodies for hundreds of years, and we've liberated those same bodies from them. But to what end? There has been much speculation. Well, this is your room."

We came to a stop. At first glance this chamber had little to recommend it. Moonlight slanted onto a mattress bordered by dust balls and crates piled upon crates. "What's in there?" I asked.

"Tools my granddaughter has collected," our host said.

"Really?"

"Yes, she thought she'd make herself useful in doing odd repairs around this old house. Why are you smiling?"

"Tools," I repeated. "This could be interesting. Asante, oh hooded one." I left his moldering shroud in the hall to do some exploring.

Day Four: A Debt He Can Never Repay

JAMAI SLEPT ON THE FLOOR IN A DORMITORY area, probably a community sleeping area for the disciples of Elias in the days when this house was still operational. No bunks remained. Anyway she seemed to prefer sleeping on a hard surface.

She'd found some of her grandfather's old clothes. He must've been a tall fellow. The long coat and outrageous length of scarf around her neck draped her completely. As I watched, Jamai's breath whistled beneath a floppy broad-rimmed hat. I tried stroking her hair, as stiff and greasy as it was. I was probably doing more harm than good. I settled beside her on my haunches instead.

"I never told you about my brother," I whispered. "One of our family's troubling secrets… it's not a subject we care to bring up. Too many unpleasant memories, especially for Mother. I sometimes forget he existed… not surprising, since he… well, we're not sure what happened to him."

She moaned softly in her sleep. Somehow it was easier to speak of such things when she was asleep. "His name was Goukoni. He'd been taken from us at a conference in Eritrea. Actually it wasn't far from the area where Ahela…"

Damn. Why was I even bringing this up? They were gone, both of them. We had no family, either of us. What good would this meandering in the past accomplish? I left Jamai to rest and went back to the pending business.

Our purloined skiff held a cartridge box full of a lively assortment of shraper shells. I'd managed to engrave three of them with the pentagram symbol Ngojama seemed to dread. I hoped to encode a few more before my eyes burned out of my skull.

"Insomnia, hmm?"

My fingers jerked as our host wafted through a wall. I ignored a sudden cramp in my wrist and shook my head. He continued, "I could simulate a counter-current in your cerebellum to induce sleep."

"No! I mean, asante, no."

"Are you afraid I'll alter your mind?"

"Yes, now that you mention it."

The spirit chuckled. The subtle echo of his humor from every wall didn't induce any more relaxation. "I need to alter more of these projectiles before I can sleep," I said.

His orbs glowed bluish-white inside his hood. "Isn't that risky? If the shraper casing disengages, there may be a catastrophic weapons failure."

That was a mouthful. "I've got to risk it," I said. "I need some kind of practical defense against Ngojama."

Our host waited in the entry, hands crossed at arm's length across his front. "I cannot help. The static discharges I emit may cause a spontaneous shell rupture. My granddaughter would not be happy with me for that."

"I know, Great Elder, asante."

"You don't have to call me that."

"Yes, but it gives me emotional comfort."

He left me to my work after that. It wasn't that easy to breach the shell's molecular bonding. Those bonds would normally be loosened by the high velocity the pellets achieved in shooting down the launch tube. Under the intense friction they'd finally shatter before reaching their target. Still, these were deadly dangerous toys. I intended to proceed with utmost caution.

I'd managed another pair of shrapers before... well, I curled up on the floor snoozing. Luckily the thing I'd been working on rolled harmlessly into a fold of carpet.

A warm and spicy scent overpowered the crumbled plaster stench. The overhead lights threw a twilight glow over the chamber. On a tool crate facing me sat a steaming bowl of couscous with a spoon standing upright in the middle. Tucked into the curve of the bowl was a folded note: *Rafiki, follow the arches.*

What was this bloody nonsense about? I'd mouthed down my third spoonful before I noticed the arched sketching, drawn in pink marker on the inner wall, a quarter meter from the entry. I was guessing that this was a packaged dish, judging from the limp slivers of peppers scattered through the rice. Nonetheless I appreciated the gesture and devoured the flavorless offering. It came with me into the hall.

I followed her crude etchings three doors down to a chamber reeking of warm adhesive. Jamai was whistling a sad tune as she fingered several sheets of wall prints. Glue dribbled from her arms and cheeks, while another glob had solidified in the bangs over her right eye.

"Hullo." I ventured tentatively over the tarpaulins spread across the floor. She probably sensed me coming, since she only glanced my way with a smile. "I like the rainforest pattern."

"Do you think so?" she asked dubiously. "It's probably not dignified enough for a house of Elias."

He's not very likely to complain about it now, is he? I bit down the thought, like so many before it, and advanced over eggshells. "I don't think he'd mind a little color."

She found that agreeable. I mounted the laser-point level; she pasted the wall print relatively straight. Never mind the many wrinkles in the print. It certainly livened up the room. "Where did this come from?" I asked, hefting the black laser tool.

"Same place as the others," she said, nodding to the lockboxes piled below the trestles near the wall behind us. "Baba is fond of a supplier north of the Sipi Falls. He still accepts payments from Baba's credit account, even when it's given through a… proxy."

"That's the other thing, how did you move all this?" A stubby mahuti trundled through the entry. It placed a fresh canister of glue in her hands and rumbled out the archway again.

I stared after it. "Isn't that the mahuti that always tended your father's garden?"

"Yes," she murmured. "I found it waiting for me one time under the sacred tree with one of your parents' care packages. There was no message attached, but… I could guess where it came from."

I slipped the canister from her hand and put my food tray down on top of it. Unexpectedly she stepped back from me. "Why are you staring at me that way?"

"What… I wasn't…"

"Yes you were! You still are, like… like I was something special. The way you always have, since…" Both her hands braced her skull as she slumped to the wall. I followed her down. Thanks be, she allowed me to stroke her cheek.

"You don't remember, do you?"

"Remember what? What is it I'm supposed to remember?"

"The greatest gift you ever gave us."

"It was May, during the Long Rains. The skies had been darkened for weeks while the lizards filled the walls in our loft. The never-ending patter of rain on the roof only added to our torture. Mother had been confined to her bed for six weeks. Out of all of us, she'd taken the death of Ahela the hardest. She'd been her light since my brother Goukoni had passed on, and to have lost her, too… Mother alternated between terrifying keening and mammoth rage at my father.

"In spite of his own grief, Father never lashed out at my mother. She'd been traveling with him in Ethiopia; perhaps he believed he was guilty also. I'd been with Mother most of this time. I was afraid of leaving her, afraid she was going to die too. And then you came. You hadn't been out of your house for weeks either, as far as anyone knew.

"You were barely seven years old, all skin and bones, and you told everyone to leave. And they did. Nobody paid me any mind; I was lying on a pile of blankets on Father's side of the bed where I could be close to Mother. I saw you climb onto the bed with her. Mother seemed to calm down for the first time in weeks. You were both in some kind of trance. I remember the room cooled. Then a slight breeze wafted through the room, ruffling through the curls in your hair.

"Mother kept watching you. Then you came to her and gave her a hug. I was right there with my nose hanging over the mattress, but you two were in your own little world. The sorrow lines began to smooth over Mother's face. I don't know what you did, but you saved her. You gave me back my mother, and the wife back to my father.

"After a while you tucked her in and lay across her back. An hour later you went home. Mother got up and had a heart-to-heart with my father. The pain was still fresh, but now we could bear it. In a matter of days, she had eased back into her life teaching at the village nursery."

"I know. The rains that year began on the day Ahela died," Jamai whispered. "I don't know how I knew what to do. I… I just put her in touch with all the life around us… all the energy I touched every single day. I wanted her to know she was loved, and we needed her, and I… I didn't want you to lose your mother, too."

"You did. Oh yes, you did. Now let me help you. Come with me. Let's settle this business with Jomoro and leave this place."

"Where are we supposed to go?"

I took her hand. "Do you remember last fall after the harvest? We talked about starting a new tradition together."

"As what, traveling bandits?"

"There's another aspect you're not considering," I pointed out. "So it's true you're cut off from the home and family you've always known. Don't you see that makes us free?"

"Free?" She stared at me like I'd grown three heads. "You have a strange sense of humor. How is this supposed to make me free? I have no place to go."

"What do you suggest, going back to that pile of dirt we call home? They've abused you from the day you were born! If they're that anxious to toss you to the wind, I say grant their wish! Damn it, Kukuwazuka, we can finally start our life together."

She matched my gaze with bright eyes, then slowly detached her fingers from mine. "What life? What about you? What about your schooling? We'd be starting with nothing. Sweet Ngai, you can't ask me to burden you that way."

"Will you listen to me? Just once, will you consider the possibilities, instead of the negatives? I could've picked anyone to be my bride, and I have. I've chosen you."

"No… no, I can't. Rafiki, please, you don't know what I've done."

"Oh come on, I know about the Poppy Girls."

"That's not what I meant."

"Supposing I do know? Why can't you trust me?"

Usually from this type of conversation I can expect one of two responses. She'll either curl up in a ball or I could get rapped with her bony knuckles. I thought I might get a bit of both routines as her mouth worked furiously. She chose to draw up her knees and slump over them. I didn't think I stood to lose anything at this point, so I kept talking.

"I understand it'll be difficult, but others have started with less. I won't cut you off from your family, but you have to realize that, apart from your grandmother, you have no family. We're free to start our own, just as our ancestors have done for countless generations."

"Yes, well… there's one crime I can't be absolved from."

"Kukuwazuka, we can't hide here forever. Won't you even consider what I'm suggesting?"

She rocked in her little ball, tapping her index finger on her knee. She bobbed her head, then lifted another wall print from the floor. We decorated another couple of walls, with about as much expertise as before, until it was time for us to trudge to our respective rooms for the night.

Day Five: The Gift of the Dead

"As far as spirits go, it's always helpful if there is a tangible connection, either to that person's home or a distant relation. If one is especially gifted…"

"Or especially innocent…"

"Yes, well, in that case, perhaps the desire is enough to satisfy at least an anthropomorphic need… to bond with an animal familiar, or two, as the case may be."

"Yes, right."

"Our histories," the Morathi added, "tell us that the period following the Genocidal Wars was one where many people sought solace in alternate forms of worship. No doubt this came about because traditional faiths had failed in satisfying the spiritual needs of their congregations. The promotion of the wars by these same religions also had the effect of shattering people's faith in the promises that were betrayed by tradition."

He found me outside this morning. Jamai had assured me that Ngojama would be inactive in the daytime, and I thought I'd better put the time to good use. I had been rummaging through the skiff's onboard mainframe trying to disable whatever GPS signal might be broadcast through it.

The Morathi reached across my elbow and fazed through the dash. Sparks crackled around my arm. I jerked myself away as a sharp ozone stench clawed at my eyeballs. "There, job done," he muttered. "Come back inside."

I didn't want to go back inside. The silence had become an insurmountable burden. At least in Baba Elgonyi, one had the distant bickering of vendors at the market to listen to, or the totos laughing on Public School playgrounds. This so-called "temple" couldn't even boast the subtle buzz of a home generator. A tomb offered more ambiance.

Her grandfather was using the free time we had to explain certain aspects of the Children of Sydelle to me. For my part I was trying very hard to ignore Jomoro's shrieking, which vibrated throughout my initializer.

"Concurrently these same institutions exhibited a fanatical conservatism not seen since the medieval period in Europe. Whole congregations engaged in witch-hunts directed against any group or individual perceived as a threat to the moral well-being of the community. It was into this hotbed of conflict and disbelief that the Ancient Order of Elias was born.

"Elias wouldn't have given his group such a pretentious name; it's doubtful he'd have named it at all. He never even bothered with registration forms… safer for his wards, you see. Anyone in need was welcome to come and go as they pleased, although, due to the nature of the times, this entailed going at their own risk.

"Elias took it upon himself to gather any gifted children to his mansion for shelter, and among these was a young lady named Sydelle. Like so many teens she was plagued by feelings of loneliness and inadequacy, and acutely aware of the difference her power granted her. She latched onto him like a thirsty child. Elias made many promises in those days; he was good-hearted by nature. His difficulty often lay in the follow-through. Possibly if he'd delegated more responsibility… but that wasn't in his nature, either.

"He directed Sydelle at uneven intervals," the Morathi continued, "but other tasks demanded his attention. Saving libraries, smuggling the gifted to other safe houses. This may have gone on for months, or only weeks; the records do not say. It isn't hard to see that Sydelle might have grown tired of his constant but well-meaning put-offs.

"She took the initiative to ransack Elias' considerable library to study ancient lore, Druidism, and the like. Nobody knows what book finally destroyed her as a mortal. Elias burned the volume, the only one he is known to have done so. Of this we are certain: she managed to wedge open a crack into another... dimension... it's hard to describe the unknown, you know."

"Umm-hmm," I said, just to keep the conversation going. "Does Jamai know this?"

"Know it? She is the one who uncovered these facts on my behalf."

"I see. Go on."

"A physical bridge was not necessary, as we are dealing with creatures without substance. You or my granddaughter, for example, could never cross over to their realm, since you both have mass and substance. But Sydelle had contacted a being from a shadow world where consciousness is diluted among its members. Contact with a single human mind was needed to concentrate an individual spirit's will. This creature bargained, convincingly it would seem, that if Sydelle would channel his spirit through her material form, she would stand to gain all of his knowledge of the dark arts. In this way, she would gain mastery of her gifts in the shortest possible time.

"After so many years of fumbling blindly along, it must have seemed an attractive offer. The bargain was sealed with six drops of blood in a brazier of incense."

"That hardly seems adequate to the task," I commented. "How much of this is fact?"

"There lies the problem Many facts could have changed in the intervening 500 years. I only know it is the story my granddaughter recovered in her file searches. As the tale goes, the spell of summoning was incanted before the hour of midnight. The ritual itself may have had no meaning, other than as a means for Sydelle to focus herself. But apparently she'd failed to take the precaution of placing wards around her summoning circle to protect herself. Sydelle opened herself to her supposed benefactor, and he absorbed her."

I waited a beat, but the Morathi appeared momentarily distracted by the husky singing emanating two floors below us. "What's that supposed to mean?" I prompted.

He swirled to fix me with sad orbs as blue as superheated metal. "Channeling is an iffy concept at best. What Sydelle achieved was a superposition, whereby two thought processes merge within one host body. But because of their incompatibility, the composition of one atomic structure differing from the other, the host may be subject to physical mutation. Now when I say absorbed, young man, I mean it in the most literal sense. The soul of Sydelle was consumed by this spirit creature, her body overshadowed by that spirit which she'd summoned."

"What… what did she mutate into?" I asked.

The shroud shrugged. "Who's to say? The records are silent on that point. This shadow immediately killed two of Elias' wards, including a young man not much older than yourself, with whom Sydelle had been very much in love. A new sect was born of these events, the Children of Sydelle, in order to bring others of its kind into our dimension.

"She warned Elias of this very thing, that her first priority would be to throw open the inter-dimensional gate and release her brothers from their captivity. Not a terrible goal in and of itself, but the means they have used… Sydelle herself was essential to this plan, or at any rate the raw talent that she possessed, which was in the hands of some nether fiend. They were unable to banish this creature back to its native dimension, referred to as a sphere. But, using the same lore as that unfortunate child, Sydelle, had for her summoning, Elias and six of his followers trapped her between electromagnetic wards and cast her mind into a catatonic state.

"Sydelle's defiled body was encased in amber, so the records say, and hidden on an uncharted island known only to ourselves. But since that time the seas have risen and islands had vanished beneath the waves. Maps change in 500 years, even coastlines. The seas have begun to recede, but it is still uncertain exactly where Sydelle's mortal shell lies hidden.

"For the last 500 years, the Children of Sydelle have sought her body in order to restore her, so that she may direct them in their grisly task. Only the highest-ranking priests of her order and ours know the total truth, which you now are privy to. Over that time her children have fed her countless spirits, always the innocent, as you have seen. Her order has remained small, usually numbering in the dozens, but it has persisted... excuse me?"

I'd been talking over the top of him. "Sorry," I said. "Host bodies. Suddenly it's all clear. You said Sydelle was needed to open the barriers? Those bodies they've been storing in amber, that's what they're for. *Vessels*, she called them. Sydelle needed to take possession of a host body in order to use her gift to free her brothers."

"Even as Auflauring intended for her to take possession of my granddaughter," our host nodded. "As the newly crowned leader of the Children of Sydelle, she could be the one to part the dimensions at each outpost where her disciples were keeping those poor wretched husks. The dead would be filled with the consciousness of all her brother spirits still trapped in limbo."

Her husky voice broke into our briefing, rising in song:

I have waited so many nights / the stars still mock my desires / no name 'mong our honored kin / no spoor to lead through the long grass...

Her timorous tone faded as it gained in strength. "Interesting," the Morathi said. "That's not what she was singing before. Shall we?"

His spectral hand rose, glowing in the pitch dark. Side-by-side we hurried along a firm, carpeted hallway. "More of her refurbishments?" I asked.

He grunted, "Hmm-hmm," and no more.

The song led us deeper inside this temple:

I had waited for your return / crawled on my belly just to be near / my days only offered solitude, / the night was filled with silences...

"It's changed? What the bloody hell had she been singing before?" I demanded.

"Primarily recriminations against herself. Shall I elaborate?"

"I'll take your word."

The song took on an undercurrent of yearning as we neared a metallic escalator. At the foot of this dead structure lay heaps of abrasive pads. Streaks and pocks of rust in its slats testified to her scrubbing efforts.

How could I have been so wrong / knowing the taste of your heart? / Lying in your lion's embrace / I could almost believe in myself...

"I need to go on alone," I said. "I have one last gift for her." The Morathi had no objections, and waved me on. I quickened my pace.

I found her in what must have once passed for a library. The book racks were tumbled over each other, some with the shelves detached from their mounts. Most were horizontal, one atop the other on the floor. A fine glossy powder crunched underfoot around the blobs of former workstations. I exhaled a chill breath as it occurred to me that the powder might once have been information discs.

Jamai slumped with her back to one of those lumps, her knees tucked up to her chin. She was tossing a small glass cube back and forth between her hands. I squatted down to stare at nothing with her. "*Hodi*," I said.

It was difficult to read her expression through the mass of curls spilling over her cheeks. "*Mzuri sana*, Rafiki," she lied. Well, we both knew things were not fine.

She probably could have sat all day meditating, but I couldn't stand one second more of this silence. "I brought you something from Nairobi," I said, reaching into my pocket, "a final gift from Li Shun."

She snatched it from me before I could make her feel any more guilty and popped the catch. The compact's lid slowly tipped open. A pale azure light scanned her eyes, and a prime mahuti's voice pronounced, "Subject identified. Access to data stream approved."

As she held it at arm's length, red neon letters scrolled in the air over her lap. A frown creased her brow, but the compact's neutered voice continued. "Subject, Jamai Fatima Dlamini. Father, Siboniso Dlamini, biologist, Sahara Reclamation Project Generation 4 out of 11 projected. birthplace, Baba Elgonyi. Mother, Fatima Nouari. birthplace, Somaliland…"

"Mama…?" Jamai's eyes moistened. She tracked the neon text, silently mouthing the words. "Fatima… Baba gave me her name…"

I'd been leaning in to tap the repeat prompt. The compact scolded me, saying, "You are not the authorized party. Request denied." I started to prompt Jamai to give the command, whereupon it repeated, "I said, you are not authorized."

Jamai spoke in a reverential whisper. "How did you...?"

"Li Shun had been saving the information on a stand-alone hard drive since our visit to the Masai Mara. He said your father wanted you to have it, in case anything happened to him."

I trailed off at the misty glaze with which she regarded the gift. Her fingers traced the edges of the compact. "I'd... I meant to give it to you four days ago, but with all that's happened... and then you socked me in the mouth... twice..."

"Grandfather!"

I shuddered at her cry. She flashed to her feet and bounded to meet her spirit relative at the hall where I'd entered this wreckage. They exchanged a few brief remarks, and then he stuck a finger into the compact's projection lens, up to and past the second knuckle. "Hey-hey-hey!" I bellowed.

"Do relax, young man," he admonished. "There is no electromagnetic activity on my part. I'm simply extracting the pertinent information. There," he said to Jamai. "This won't take long, now that I know..."

"Asante, Grandfather," she grinned, rocking on her heels as he departed. With that done she skipped back to my side. She shook her head sadly and pushed my jaw shut.

"Dear Rafiki, I've been so remiss. All this time and you've barely caught a glimpse of this house. Elias would not have approved." She took my hand in hers and said, "Come, let me show you around."

I don't know what she expected me to see. The architectural style was typical of 21st century thinking, bland, ordinary, and without a great deal of imaginative design. The walls were uniformly flat with faux candle fixtures mounted at head-height. The texture was not unlike sandstone, rough and far too porous to the touch. It was a wreck, though this time I refrained from saying so out loud.

She claimed to have raided her father's credit to cover such bolts of red velvet carpet as she'd been able to lay thus far. As for the walls, one could discern paler swatches where tapestries, long deteriorated, had once hung. "Elias believed in plainness," Jamai explained as she led me along a seemingly endless corridor.

"He certainly put that ethic to work here," I muttered.

She ignored the crack. "Ostentation displays an arrogance much too common in the Lost Age. The spiritually hungry have no need of distractions."

This floor seemed to follow a hexagonal pattern, one flat wall ending in a sharp corner that angled off to the next one. After one sharp turn, three corners in, we ducked into a maintenance closet tucked between two support braces. Jamai blew a high-pitched whistle. The self-charging cooler just inside the door chucked two half-liter drinks from the circular port in its lid.

"Inshallah, Rafiki," she toasted. I mumbled something indistinct and tapped my drink to hers. She also offered me a bowl of homemade manioc and beans. Even though it was as tasteless as plaster, I devoured it. The long fingers of hunger still gnawed at my stomach, but at least this bland fare took the edge off my appetite. I suppose after I'd been here a few weeks, I'd be as emaciated as she was becoming.

"Rafiki," she said, taking my bowl. "You've made me recall my painful memories. It's your turn. I still don't understand why you're up on charges. What happened to that sweet old man?"

That seemed fair enough. "I needed his help. Given the mutual interest he seemed to share with your father, I assumed there were things he could tell me about your parents. Why else would your father have sent you to see him at the Halls of Shame, a year ahead of your school age? We started by contacting the Resources Department at the Masai Mara Reserve."

"We... being you and your father?" I nodded. "When did you do this?"

I shrugged sheepishly. "About six weeks before I left for university. I explained to the Reserve that I was a former student, that we'd once visited that old Masai museum, the Halls of Shame, and could they put us in touch with this nice old man, etcetera etcetera. The staff was happy to oblige. He'd worked as a groundskeeper at the university until his retirement several rains past. He lived at a cottage east of the campus."

"Did he remember you?"

"Not exactly. All I know is, I walked through his door and he shouted 'Hi-yahh!'"

She tried to pretend to grimace, but I could see the corners of her lips curving. "He karate-chopped you? What for?"

"That's what I asked after he helped me off the floor." I let her have her laugh; she'd had little enough of that lately. Then I resumed my narrative. "He had to verify my handprint on his palm-reader, and he apologized. He said he had to be certain I wasn't an agent of Sydelle's group. While he served sweet tea, he explained that he knew about the kiama, that's why he chopped me. He said everyone associated with you was in danger. I reminded him about that crack he made at the museum, about him and your father. I believed he wanted us to follow up on that, and there I was."

"Was that the only time you met him?"

I shook my head. "We met three times after that, the last two times at his tea house out in the garden. We tossed old stories back and forth. I told him what I could about you, and he prepared that compact I gave you. Did you know he'd been carrying on a long correspondence with your father?"

"But... I saw Baba's correspondence," Jamai said. "He relied on me to file his important messages in a separate inbox and dispose of the rest."

"That's where they were clever. They directed their messages to your father's Eritrean headquarters for the SRP. Their IDs were disguised using alternate pseudonyms. They even used an oblique collection of idiomatic phrases to get their messages across. It worked well enough for the last eleven years to fool Sydelle's fisis."

"So you got everything you wanted from him."

"Yes. for all the good it did him. At our last meeting he asked me to return in two days. He'd uncovered information that would overturn everything we knew about Sydelle. I hid the compact in a security box at the speed-rail station just off the student commons."

"What did he want to tell you?" she asked with bright eyes.

"I don't know... that was the day I found his body, and the police fell all over me."

"You didn't touch the murder weapon?" When I winced, she had all the answer she needed. "Rafiki, his mind...they didn't...?"

"I don't think so. Jomoro said there'd been no internal brain damage like there had been with the other victims... couldn't have been." I started to laugh; there wasn't any other way to deal with the madness of the situation. "His head had been beaten into a blob of meat, and someone took a machete to his body…" I couldn't elaborate on the grislier details; sweet Ngai, I wish I could forget them. "I led them to him."

A short sharp tap of her fingers on my cheek brought me back to my senses. "You don't know that, Rafiki!"

"Well it was a most interesting coincidence, wasn't it? They'd never have found him if I hadn't been nosing around… *samahani, samahani*, I shouldn't have shouted…"

She hadn't pulled away this time. Her arms opened and enfolded me in a gentle embrace. We rocked quietly in that dim room, Ngai knew for how long. Then she disengaged and eased to her feet. Holding out her hand she whispered, "Rafiki, come."

We raced through a maze of tunnels to a candle-lit chamber. Whatever furnishings that had once been here had long since returned to the dirt. Braces still hung from the high ceiling, however, while a heap of metal supports lay piled carelessly at the far wall amid a pile of sweepings. Freshly woven mats with a recurring butterfly theme covered a small area of floor.

"Elias' people used this as a gymnasium to limber up after hours of study and meditation," Jamai said. "On occasion it had other uses."

"Kukuwazuka, are you sure about this?" But she was finally putting her power to good use. Her arms rose, crossing over her head. Her trunks crinkled as they peeled away, exposing her neck and collarbone. Yes, well, basically it slipped off her shoulders. She arched sinuously as though she were sliding free of a second skin.

Her bright jade eyes shone with trepidation and desire. As for myself, I had my own inner conflict. Traditionally either of us could be ostracized for what we were about to do. Under present circumstances I don't suppose that mattered. The larger issue, at least as far as I saw, was whether we dared lose our self-control at all.

The sexually transmitted plague that began in the late 20th Century killed millions of my brothers. My father, indeed all our village Elders, had drilled these facts into our skulls since we were schoolboys. Millions of boys such as ourselves had been made orphans. Worse still, the entire Plague of Flies, as we called it, was facilitated by my gender's lack of control. Their dumbsticks had been my brothers' downfall.

Our Elders had assumed a more mature sexual attitude. Unfortunately, I hadn't foreseen this circumstance. I was more interested in bringing her back alive. My father's teachings placed the burden of responsibility on me. Besides which, her father would probably kill me if I took advantage of her.

Fortunately, my Father had anticipated this. Before my departure, he'd instructed S'manga Nlebela to apply an SI-patch where it'd do the most good. While Father and Jomoro stood by with crossed arms, S'manga explained that the patch would release a cocktail of sexually inhibiting chemicals. It would continue to act for eight days, long enough to find her and, additionally, to control my hormones. Now I only had to convince Jamai to do the same.

She was reluctant at first. After I explained that it didn't mean that I didn't desire her, she yanked the V-tails of her skirt between her thighs and tucked them into the sash around her waist. All I had to do now was to keep from ripping them both off her. Simple.

She sang, "I have waited so many nights…"

"Shh."

Of all the impressions of that first time… hands kneading soft flesh… lips touching…

Day Six: All Her Rage Pouring Out

WELL, YOU DIDN'T EXPECT ME TO TELL EVERYTHING? What we'd done was a healthy expression of our intimate feelings. In the traditions of our people it is a sacred act, done in a well-regulated manner.

The afternoon found us still entwined. Jamai snuggled like a babe to my chest, her arms clutching me tightly. Father's patch had worked quite well, damn him. No matter what my passions desired, the dreaded *uume* remained droopy.

It was in this spirit that her grandfather barged in on us. Our hairs pricked on our arms as he loomed over our mats. He never commented either, discounting the sudden "Ooh!" as he swerved away. From across his spectral shoulder he addressed Jamai. "T-t-toto," he stammered, "it is time."

"And the circle of life marches on," I grumbled. Jamai rose quietly, unashamed of her nakedness, and shrugged into her garments. She'd never had much sense of discomfort about such things. I'd dressed too, but he blocked my path with a gently upraised palm. "It's all right, Grandfather," she said. "I want him to come."

Along with the tightness in her voice there was an equal tightening in her biceps, a bunching of her shoulder blades. "What are you two on about?" I asked.

The Morathi replied, "We're about to see her mother."

"Are we talking about her *mother* mother?" I demanded. "Not snakes or butterflies or some other creature masquerading as such?"

"I do not joke about family, boy," her grandfather said. "When I say a visitation from such-and-such a person is imminent, I speak the literal truth."

The narrow corridor we'd been traipsing along was lit by anachronistic fluorescent tubes. These probably dated to the period when this relic was originally constructed. The sandstone walls appeared smooth and dust-free, almost as though they'd been pressure-washed. No compressed air equipment was evident, although powder residue lined the edging at our feet. I suppose it was possible in the absence of available tools that Jamai simply "put her mind to it".

"She never spoke of anything like this before," I said. "I think that I'd remember that. When did this come up?"

The specter appeared surprisingly sheepish on this point, going so far as to cough over his answer. I insisted that he repeat it. "Actually," he admitted, "it was my idea."

"Yours!" I hissed.

"Well you weren't here to be any help." In spite of the well-up of anger, I hung my head. I was as guilty as anyone of holding back the truth, maybe more than most. Still, her grandfather seemed to regret that sharp rejoinder and hurriedly apologized. We paused outside a chamber as he explained.

"It had seemed the best thing at the time," he said. "She had nowhere else to turn. The first week in this temple she spent moping inside this chamber. I had to give her something tangible to hope for. Being that the mind is electromagnetic in nature, and that the soul, also electromagnetic, is just another form of energy…"

"Yes yes, and energy can never be created or destroyed, but only change form." I dug my knuckles into both eyes. These physics discussions always bent my head in school. His assumptions were no less ludicrous. I lowered my hands and faced him directly. "And you think you've accomplished this?"

His orbs glowered orange around what appeared to be hazel pupils. "I have," he proclaimed like a schoolboy. "Contact was achieved Saturday night. She has agreed to meet with Jamai this afternoon, in about... oh dear, we'd better get in there." His musty robes flapped into my nostrils as we bustled into the chamber.

The room was a more impressive sight than other places I'd seen in this house. Fresh mahogany panels had been fitted to every wall, up to arm's length at any rate. Chandeliers glistened with crystal radiance, a ring of candles in every fixture. The floor had deteriorated to bare concrete, but an orderly succession of postholes showed clearly where the benches or pews once belonged.

Face-forward at the head of the chamber stood a lectern on a hexagonal platform, twelve centimeters above the main floor. It covered a four-meter radius where Jamai paced wringing her hands. Behind her hung a tapestry bearing the image of some Euro in a dinner jacket and a host of totos of varying nationalities at his feet.

"Elias?" I muttered. The specter nodded and crossed himself.

The hair on my arms began to rise as a static tingle preyed on my skin. Chills wafted through the aisles. Once, twice, a breeze blew, though there was no outlet from here to the outside world. Jamai edged to the right-hand border of her stage, mouth aquiver as a shape detached itself from the wall.

The flowing burnoose couldn't disguise all of that spirit's curves. I guessed she'd been slender in her former life. Reddish bands in varying widths and hues delineated her dark crimson garb. Pelican-like hands peeled back the hood from a thin face whose eyes seemed too round for the head where they were set. The spirit smiled, extending her right hand. The sight was extraordinary; apart from the smile, the two of them might have been a mirror for each other.

Jamai managed a feeble, "Mama?"

"Yes, child." Warmth permeated our visitor's subdued contralto tones. "It is I. I am your mother."

In that moment, I felt very warm towards Jamai's grandfather. This was one thing I could never have given her. Though it'd seemed the most asinine suggestion when first I heard it, in truth it was probably the best thing that could've happened. Any moment now the spell of silence would be broken. Any moment she'd rush to her mother's arms. Any... time... now.

Why was she just standing there?

Jamai stared at the proffered hand. No, wait, she was positively glaring. A small frown tugged at the spirit's mouth. Then she lowered her palm. "Child," she prompted, "I'm here. There must be questions you wish answered."

"Yes," Jamai hissed. She should have been happy. This was her life's dream, wasn't it? So why were her shoulder muscles tensing? As she stepped forward, her strong hands balled into fists. "I want to know why you abandoned me."

Her grandfather and I exchanged dismayed glances. Perhaps even a spirit can be discomfited. She glanced at the paneling, the murals, everywhere but at Jamai. "Child, the choice was never mine. If I..."

"Liar! You could have stopped them! You could have made them leave me alone! Why did you leave me, you bitch?"

She took two running steps and pounded on her mother's bosom. Her grandfather and I were too dumbfounded to move. Whatever impulse should have stirred us to action seemed to have stunned us into immobility instead. All these years I'd had my own expectations of how such a meeting might have gone. I never dreamed of this.

While her fists blurred, Jamai's cries became shriller. The anger dispelled quickly enough, at least. Her knees gave way and she slid to the floor clutching her mother's hem. "You didn't have to leave me," she sobbed. "You could have stopped them."

The spirit stole a glance in our direction. We ducked behind opposite support beams. She'd forgotten about us as I poked my nose around my hiding place. Now she was cupping Jamai's chin in her palm.

"You don't understand. I never abandoned you. Never."

"When?" Jamai hissed. "Where the hell were you? When were you ever with me?"

"Child, please… when you slept with the pythons, my spirit protected you."

Jamai's stare glazed over. "What…?"

"When you and Ahela sang to the butterflies, my spirit directed you. I comforted you the best I could…" Her face ducked into her delicate hands. "Oh my god, child, I couldn't touch you. I was only spirit, a conscious mind reduced to pure energy. The only time I had to hold you was on my deathbed."

"You were there… every time?"

"I couldn't let go. The only way I could hold you was to inhabit the mind of those overgrown slugs. You knew. On the most basic subconscious level, you knew. And when it was time to master your power, I guided you, through your totem, to these sacred grounds. Although," she said, raising her voice an octave, "some people were a little overzealous in their duties." Across from me, her grandfather's upper body slumped.

For my part I sagged behind my support. This certainly explained a great deal. All these years she'd been calling those things *mama*. I'd thought it was just an affectation. I never imagined there might be any basis for her sentiment. I continued listening from our hiding spot.

"Why didn't you tell me?"

"Child, would you have believed me?"

The chamber became suddenly silent. I risked a peek around my support. They were both on their knees, Jamai with her head down. "What difference would it have made?" her mother asked. "Nobody would have believed you either."

"I could've kept it to myself!"

Her mother cocked her head in the way Jamai always had. "They knew about your totems."

"Only because I fell out of a tree…"

"And Nyoka caught you. I remember. Listen, your age mates would've only had another reason to mock you. I couldn't do that to you. You weren't ready for the truth. Now, since you're old enough… but look at you, see how you've grown, young and strong… wait, child. Rise. The floor is no place for you."

She took hold of Jamai's elbows and helped her to stand. Jamai took a swing at her arm, but it was the impotent blow of a child. "What are you talking about? What truth? I needed you, not those damned totems!"

"Don't you understand? You weren't supposed to have so much power." Jamai could only stare incredulously.

"I… I'm not…? Take it away, then. I don't want it."

"Child, it's too late. It can't be done."

"Stop telling me what can't be done! You're here, aren't you! Take this damn power away from me!"

Her mother pressed two fingers to Jamai's lips to shush her. "Had your father allowed my brothers to guide you," she continued, "we could have trained you properly, safely. He never would have lost you. It'd have only been for a few hours out of every week. But he didn't want you to have any part of our conflict. And you had so much potential. Everyone has these potentials, but our schooling trains them out of us, until our disbelief takes over. My brothers would have enabled you to focus on your gift."

"B… but I can do so much. I move things with my thoughts. The grass, Mama… the grass parts to let me pass. How is that?"

"Everything else is ancillary." Her mother's voice rose for the one and only time during this entire conversation. "Without the empathic component, the ability to feel the other person's pain, you would have nothing to govern your power or the passions you got from me." Her voice softened again, and a spectral hand brushed Jamai's cheek. "Besides, you've already used it. Remember your first day in this temple, in this very room. You brought Esaias Dlamini back into the fold, back into the family. We're so very grateful for that. It's your innocence that enables you to do these things, child. Don't fear it. Embrace your inner child."

What the hell did she mean by that crack? Jamai's head had slunk to the level of her shoulders. Her hands clasped her mother's wrists, the way she'd always clutched her snakes. "The guilt… it never goes away, does it?"

"No, it doesn't in the best of persons. It's a compelling human quality."

The spirit's burnoose billowed from beneath as she gathered Jamai in another embrace. I could see the muscles tighten in Jamai's arms as she crushed the spirit to her, murmuring "*Samahani*," over and over.

"It's time I was going," her mother whispered. "I think we've covered enough ground as it is. Come back tomorrow to the receptionary. I'll meet you at the fountain. We have a lot to talk about. Remember, child, I have never left you. And I never will."

She began to drift back, back into the wings behind the lectern. Jamai clung to her hand as long as possible. Their fingers brushed, and then Jamai stood alone. I wondered where she phased to, until an icy breath whispered in my ear, "You know, one day you should tell her the truth."

Her cold presence washed through my bones. By the time I jerked around, she'd already vanished back to wherever immaterial beings go between hauntings.

Day Seven: Atoning to the Shadows

I DON'T THINK JAMAI SLEPT THAT ENTIRE NIGHT. Twice she shook me awake as we snuggled together to talk, about what, I can't recall. I'd agreed to almost everything she'd said, if only to end the conversation sooner. We ate our nutrient bars in silence and whiled away a few hours in general house repairs.

At the appointed hour, we strolled hand-in-hand to what once passed for a reception area. Despite Jamai's best efforts there had been little restoration that even she could do. Whatever murals might have once hung there were long gone; the decorative panels themselves had left a faded brown residue on the walls.

What was left seemed impressive enough. A stone fountain awaited in the center of a 5x7-meter floor space. It was a simple affair with no statues spitting geysers, and only a round well, now dried up. Fatima Nouari was seated on the edge facing the doorway. She held her arms open and called to her daughter. Jamai smiled nervously to me. Her fingers slowly slid from mine until we both stood at arm's length. Then she let her hand drop and hurried to her mother's side.

I slumped to the ratty carpet outside the receptionary and waited. And waited. It's a custom all men grow accustomed to in their relations with women. I listened to their murmurs until the quiet tenor of their conversation put me to sleep. It was quite some time later that Jamai nudged me awake.

"We can go now." She spoke softly and hugged herself tightly. "Apparently I'm some kind of necrobiotic."

"What, you talk to dead people?" I said.

"Not exactly," she shook her head, "although it allows me that privilege." Her cheeks screwed up appropriately. "My empathic sense appears to be attuned to the terminally ill."

"You can tell when somebody's about to die?" She nodded. "What kind of a sick gift is that? What good can come from it?"

"Mama calls it a gift of comfort. It may have been what I was doing with your mother so many rains ago. It's intended to help the dying, to be with them in their final hours, or to help speed them on their way."

"Or to give hope to the grieving," I added, "by reconnecting them to the wider Web of Life all around us."

"I suppose so. Look, the point is that the symptoms can only be relieved by doing something. It's all in Elias' diary."

"And you have that, here?"

We'd begun to stroll along the yellow-lit corridor toward the vine-covered foyer. "Every house of Elias has a copy. The original diary, if it still exists, is probably still in Old California. He filled pages with notations on every pupil. One person in particular possessed symptoms very similar to mine."

"Please tell me that wasn't Sydelle."

"Would you stop jumping ahead? No, not her. Elias barely devoted three lines to her, and that was only to remark that electronic appliances invariably flatlined in her presence." She frowned. "However, in his diary he dedicated several pages to a young Italian boy named Romero. Apparently this *toto* enjoyed nothing better than doodling gruesome pictograms of zombies. At the same time, it seemed young Romero voluntarily accompanied Elias to hospices and spent hours with the elderly residents, sketching small portraits for their amusement."

"Have I seen any of these symptoms?"

Jamai kneaded her brow in the heel of her palm. "I don't know. Elias' pupil suffered from moodiness, sluggishness, a sensation of icicles spreading from the inside." She brought herself up short. "You can stop nodding any time now."

"You haven't been wrong yet," I grinned. While she still ducked her head, she did smile. "Did your mother tell you anything else?"

"Oh yes, she told me all about how she and Baba met in Little Mogadishu. You couldn't be bothered to tell me that was one of the poorer enclaves in Nairobi."

"I didn't think casting negative aspirations on Nairobi was going to improve your mood." Nevertheless, she slipped her arm into mine and sidled close.

"Baba was an associate geneticist under a university professor at the time, on leave from the project. Mama said she lifted his wallet! She gave it back, after a whirlwind chase through the market, and over an expensive dinner that he paid for.

"Mama had been in hiding, trying to escape the clan life that her family embraced. She'd been living in a safe house under the care of a guardian of Elias. Baba didn't realize she was gifted at first, but her guardian thought they made a good couple. Little goes on in Little Mogadishu that does not get around. Somebody must have told Mama's family in traditional Mog where she'd gone. Because the next thing either of them knew, her clan Elders were chasing them both through the alleys. They might have caught them too, if Mama hadn't wrapped herself around Baba and teleported them both into the center of a Harvest dance in the village square of Baba Elgonyi."

"She… tele… she what?"

"Teleportation. That was her gift. The two of us are connected, she said, spiritually grounded by our bond as mother-daughter. That's how she could be near me whenever I left home for a… cuddle… every night."

"Aha."

"Everyone in the village dropped what they were doing. Apparently Odu Molefe's jaw unhinged in a way that would make a snake envious. Baba took it in stride. He called for the choir from Kibarenge to raise their voices. 'This is a celebration!' he cried. Mama told me that, as our spiritual leader, S'manga's father officiated at their wedding six weeks later."

We'd come to the foyer overhung by a thick tangle of liana. Her meeting with her mother must have gone longer than I imagined. An afternoon gloom darkened the entry as we passed. Two steps past the vine-covered area, Jamai backtracked, dragging me with her.

"Isn't that your skiff?" she asked.

I nodded. Of course it was; she drove us to this safe house... oh no. At the moment, its end was tipped perpendicular to the ground.

Jamai slipped through the curtain of vines before I could stop her. The ground seemed to yield for her, mulch enfolding the top of her ankle boots. She inched forward gingerly. "Careful," she called back, "the ground is much spongier now."

She tiptoed around the skiff. The restraining straps dangled over both seats, although the rear boot was still securely fastened. The pilot's seat and most of the front engine section had been swallowed by the Earth, almost as though... the Morathi and I exchanged frantic stares. As if, we both realized, it'd been sucked down by an irresistible force. "Come back! Come back now!" we both shouted.

She responded to the urgency in our voices, but her first backward step collapsed the ground around her ankles into a sinkhole a meter in diameter. She bounced clear, although the hole sucked in the surrounding mulch. Her next gingerly step was less successful. Earth and pebbles scraped into a downward funnel that Jamai instantly slid into.

Only a sharp jolt from her grandfather kept me from rushing to her side. It was just as well, since a moment later an elliptical surge of dirt erupted from the spot where she had sank. Moist clods hailed down as Jamai's body traced a backward arc over the glade. Unfortunately, when her heels bounced onto solid ground, she was even farther from the temple steps than before.

Her mouth opened in an "Oh" of astonishment a quarter-second before an earthen mound punched its way two meters to the surface. On the way up, a bluish paw closed on her wrist and yanked at her shoulder. Her screams barely covered the sudden wrench of cartilage from its socket.

I spun and blew a whistle. Jamai's toy mahuti trundled up the corridor, and all my impatient beckoning didn't get it motivated any faster. While I was loading the shraper, the outer crust of the mound poured away from Ngojama's flanks.

I almost dropped the pellets I was handling. Ice was suddenly pooling in my calves. Fortunately the glade crackled with the stench of ozone. Ngojama bellowed as Jamai's grandfather sprayed sparks across his chest. It was enough of a shock that Jamai flopped onto the grass and quickly rolled from his stamping feet.

"Oi, creature!" the Morathi taunted from behind the upturned skiff. "Here I am!"

Ngojama lashed out at him, but he'd have had better luck wrestling the wind. Its fist smashed the skiff's boot section clean off. It swerved back around, giving me the shot I needed. I took aim and fired.

Each shell impacted with a soft, moist squelch. And not much else. Ngojama gazed down at the trio of holes in its breast, dripping a pale mucous fluid. Almost at once, the holes began to fill in like dough rising from the inside. "Is that all your cheap toy is worth, boy?" it taunted.

Shit...that wasn't part of the plan! I rolled around to the other side of the archway, sweating as much from frustration as... well, anything. "What's the matter with you?" I shouted. "I thought you liked her!"

Ngojama wasn't responding. I risked a peek outside, and almost got a face-full of the tree Ngojama pitched inside the temple. Fine, then. If he was harassing me, he might be distracted from Jamai long enough for her to take shelter elsewhere.

"I do not have to explain myself to a child such as you," it growled, "nor have I any choice in what my Master requires."

"Your Master crawls with the maggots in the Underworld," I said.

Its voice assumed a mocking tone. "Oh, did you think Master Auflauring was the ultimate master of his brainless cult? He too was a tool. It was he who was given the command to capture me, in order that I might capture the Lepidopteran. My new master required his life, that he may ascend to his mistress."

While Ngojama had been monologuing, Jamai had been easing through the grass with gritted teeth, her left arm cradled tightly to her chest. She managed to push herself along on one knee, creep another few centimeters along on her good elbow, then push off on her other knee. In another couple of minutes she could crawl past Ngojama and be at the temple steps... if I could keep it talking.

"How can you still be their captive? She's smashed his crystal..."

"We've already covered this," Ngojama said wearily. "In any event, you are of no interest to me. Crawl back into the darkness like the maggot you are."

We had different ideas of what Jamai should be doing. Bracing herself on her good elbow, she pushed herself up to a handstand against Ngojama's right leg. Her legs wrapped around its knee while her right hand clawed a fist-full of hair from its massive calf.

Ngojama stared down at the appendage newly attached to its leg. "What have we?" it mocked, "a little wuolo pup come to suckle at its master's feet? Perhaps I should shake this off..." A rasp spit up through its jaws as one leg sagged. It managed a pitiful "Oh no," before it fell to one knee.

Jamai's hair began to tumble. I couldn't believe she was going to try to drain that beast. It seemed to be working, too. I hefted the shraper in my hands. Now would be the perfect time to take its head off, while it was still off balance. I scrambled over the coarse barked tree obstructing the door and dashed from the safety of Elias' temple.

I got in one swing before its paw arrested it, bare millimeters from its fangs. The sudden brake in momentum wrenched my shoulders, enabling Ngojama to pluck the shraper from my grip. It handed it back to me, straight across the jaw. I staggered in a circle while a livid pulse exploded through my face.

Two blows upside my head appeared to be enough. Ngojama struggled painfully to its feet, pausing only long enough to shrug Jamai off its massive leg. A shimmer passed between us. "Fall back!" the Morathi cried as he plunged his arm into Ngojama's chest. Right at the point where my misguided shells had impacted.

Ozone stifled our nostrils as a massive discharge crackled through its chest. Jamai and I flung ourselves on opposite sides of the surrounding hummocks as the Morathi ignited the shells. A dozen moist pops burst through Ngojama's pectorals as the shells radiated out into the grass with a dozen mosquito-like whines.

Her grandfather suddenly bellowed an order and Jamai was up. She streaked across the glade despite her injuries, and her momentum was only arrested after her right shoulder bashed into Ngojama's backside.

For the second time its body tumbled, churning a fresh path of destruction through the clearing. Now I understood exactly what the Morathi was shouting: "Drive him into the temple!"

Of course! The wards he'd had installed; if they worked as that phantom said… I called out, "Jamai! Give me a boost!"

It didn't appear as though she heard me at first; her head simply lolled in the grass. In a moment, her hair surged on a fresh billow of power, and her fists plunged into the dirt.

Well, I'd asked for it. Some massive force, like a mountain of raw hatred, slammed into my backside. Pinpricks of ice sank into every pore, and I screamed as my body soared headfirst into Ngojama. For a moment his flesh molded around my cheeks. Then it tumbled another couple of meters, and I spat the taste of rot and mud from my mouth. At least now it was hunched over the temple steps.

Swallowing because I knew full well what was coming, I shouted, "Again!"

Energy surrounded me in its icy tendrils once again. My body smashed into Ngojama, this time in its buttocks. A bellow like the crashing of jet craft roared through the glade as its belly slid along the tree, stripping vines all along its length until we both tumbled inside Elias' temple.

I rolled to one side, but caution was no longer necessary. A violent convulsion jerked Ngojama's limbs. Spasms slapped its back continually into the floor as perspiration mingled with the discolored blood shot in multiple spurts from its chest. Its pupils shrank to black points as the irises shone white. It continued these convulsions as Jamai staggered in.

Her legs wobbled like sticks in a tumbler, her left arm hanging useless at her side. Both her eyes were swollen red. Beneath those eyes a mottled discoloration already was surfacing. Her good, bloodied right hand clutched at her throat as she stared vacantly at Ngojama's writhing mass.

"Well done," her grandfather said. "Both of you. These are sacred grounds. As I told your young man, the wards are turning his negative psychic energy back onto himself, with double the intensity."

"He'll die," she said listlessly.

"Good!" I thrust the shraper into her good hand. "Finish it."

What was the matter with her? She made no move to take it. "Just take it and fill its skull with shrapnel," I said. "Do it, before it comes back after us."

Her eyelids shuttered as her teeth chattered. In her bloodshot gaze burned an emerald fire. She dropped to one knee and tugged at its paw. "Are you insane?" I bellowed. "What the fuck are you doing?"

"I am ending this, this whole stupid bloody cycle. I won't have any more blood on my hands. Help me carry him outside."

"He tried to kill us."

"Shut up and help me carry him outside!"

Maybe I'd taken leave of my own senses. I began to wonder even while I tossed my shraper across the hall. "You're mad," I grunted as we heaved Ngojama to a sitting position. Between us we each took a man-sized arm on our shoulders. "Those bugs have chewed the last morsel from your brains."

"Why are you helping then?" she sweated through gritted teeth.

"Mind-rot must be contagious."

It was no easy task. We swayed as its weight swung us from side to side. The Morathi stared from one to the other of us. What could I do but shrug? When one associates with this girl, one accepts the absurd with some alacrity.

Ngojama's bulk crashed to the brush outside the temple entry. Its great arms dragged us down on top of it. Jamai held out a trembling hand. "Let me have that artifact you're always carrying."

I gave her my knife with reservations, but without comment. "I've spared your spirit from the fire," she said, "Ngai knows why. I'm going to release you from your bondage, provided you crawl back to the Tana foothills and never return. Do you understand me?"

Its paw snaked around her left hand, swallowing most of her forearm into the bargain. Jamai waved me off even as the flesh around its grip paled. Her eyelids squeezed shut, tears spilling onto its chest. A harsh rasp hissed between her teeth as the creature rumbled, "Why? Why do you spare me?"

Jamai bit her lip to shut out the pain. A drop of blood bubbled on her upper lip. "I don't want to be a murderer," she sobbed, her voice growing huskier by the moment. "I can't live with all this blood in my thoughts, in my sleep… and… because… you were there. Even though you kept me in the dankest holes in the earth, you never left me."

The paw dropped to its side, though the imprint of its palm was grooved into her forearm. Ngojama stared skyward, intoning, "I swear by Holy Ngai and Dark Iblis that your people will never know me or mine again. Proceed, Lepidopteran."

I didn't think she could do it. Her face flushed as the tip of the blade indented the edge of the brand. Tears pooled around her tight-shut lids. Then she thrust the blade in.

Ngojama thrashed beneath her, very nearly throwing her off. I threw myself across its midsection, which wasn't that much more of a restraint. Jamai wailed savagely with its first buck, but it settled down. Her mane covered the fresh wound she'd inflicted. She lifted her head and began sawing.

The knife was ill suited for the job. She was only doing it by sheer muscle. Her fist tightened knuckle-white as it cut around the brand. Then she inclined the blade and dug beneath the circle of flesh.

Soon it was done. She flung the bloody chunk of flesh into the nearby brush, then slumped across Ngojama's prickly haired chest. For some minutes they lay panting together, its massive arm across her back. At her grandfather's urging, I gently rolled her off. Ngojama in turn rolled onto its stomach and touched its brow to the Earth.

I still don't understand the displacement process. I can only report that the moist Earth ground into a widening radius around its skull. Into this fresh hole, Ngojama wriggled its vast bulk. The beast's heels pawed at the air as the dirt filled the sinkhole behind it, so that not a trace remained.

It was only at this point that I discovered she had no hand left to speak of. The organ had been crushed into a swollen mass of pulp with slivers of bone projecting through the joints and nails. With Ngojama gone, whatever form of compartmentalization she used to block out the pain appeared to crumble.

A sudden sharp shriek tore from her throat. Her right hand clawed at the mulch as the scream went on and on. There wasn't anything I could do but hold her while spasms shook her body and her eyes grew wide. Other things I began to notice, probably to distract myself from my helplessness. For one thing, that improvised GPS scrambler of mine was now frayed into strips that had been gouged several millimeters beneath the flesh of her wrist.

What I hadn't noticed were the camouflaged bodies emerging from the foliage. I counted five… ten… twenty in all. Each man braced a sharper to his shoulder, and each bore on his shoulder a badge featuring an umber hawk with wings folded obstinately over its spiked breast, the proud symbol of the East African Rangers Platoon.

After their emergence, events moved swiftly. A rifle stock exploded into my right eye-socket. While four men were detached to guard me, another dozen circled Jamai's thrashing body. Her reputation, it appeared, had more than preceded her.

They must have triangulated our position the moment that Ngojama shredded my lashed-up signal dampener. I never heard the squadron leader's name, only a rapid-fire barking of orders and accusations. I tried to tell him she was injured, that we surrendered. The squad captain smacked me and told me either to shut up or be gagged.

A corpsman knelt by her and applied a numbing spray to her arm. Someone else bustled from the bushes holding a pair of forceps before him. Ngojama's fresh-dumped brand was in their grip. Someone else pointed out the blood still damp on our hands. That some of that blood was ours didn't appear to make an impression on them.

The captain nudged my knife out of Jamai's hand with the immaculate toe of his boot. A thorough search was conducted of the immediate perimeter, but although no other bodies were found, well, one could guess what conclusions the Rangers reached.

A squad of soldiers circled the perimeter with hand telemeters, each man frowning in his own way over the odd readings they were collecting. In another minute they might be led to the temple door.

"It was Ngojama!" I squealed. The captain took this news in his stride, meaning he jammed his hand around my throat.

"He was here," I choked. "He killed Bren Auflauring, just like he killed Odu Molefe."

The fist loosened… a bit… around my neck. COBALT was the name stitched on his left breast pocket. "Where is he now?" Captain Cobalt laughed.

I pointed down to the mound of dirt we were both standing on. "That's why we've been hiding for the last three days," I said. "We were scared he'd find us."

"Four days," Cobalt corrected. "You expect me to believe you could elude us for four days? What kind of genius allowed this? Where are the signs of your habitation?"

"Please, what about Jamai?"

"Fuck her! What have you been doing here? Where is the other body? What are you hiding?"

I finally lost what little composure I had. "We're not hiding anything! How could we be hiding anything? Look at this place!" As one body, they scanned the battered shrubs and churned Earth, whose scent still filled the air. "Ngojama wiped out any sign of anything. We slept the first day away anyhow."

Cobalt stepped back and dropped his hand, which was certainly not a sign he was ready to back down. "You haven't explained why we were unable to track you. Why wasn't your skiff transmitting its transponder signal?"

"We traded up," I said. "I left my father's skiff with Auflauring's body. That's one of his floaters. I mangled the control panel so it wouldn't transmit a signal." While Cobalt detailed two men to dig around the upturned nose of the buried skiff, I added that I'd rigged a dampening shield to absorb all incoming transmissions.

"You're too stupid to devise such a thing. How…?" The captain paused as Jamai's personal mahuti poked its head above the shrubbery and offered him a fruit pouch.

"I had a little technical assistance," I replied sheepishly.

Much of that had been rubbish, but I remembered the promise Jamai had extracted from me. I intended to keep this one, for as long as I could endure their interrogation. Luckily the scans from their hand units seemed to bear out my story. I prayed part of that was some type of electrostatic field generated by her grandfather. There was nothing left for Captain Cobalt to do but shackle me and load us onto a waiting transport.

The diagnostic table at the Kibarenge Village Clinic barely accommodated Jamai's long body, even with the extension board out. Our party arrived at the emergency entrance just after midnight. Doctor Kensey wasn't able to see us until half past three. Jamai rested on my shoulder with her eyelids shuttered and a constant wheeze whistling from both nostrils.

"We have to stop meeting this way," the doctor chuckled. The last time we'd met was when Jamai was five, and he'd treated the lacerations dealt to her by the Ant totem (yes, I believe that.) His sideburns had turned a respectable shade of gray; otherwise he appeared only slightly less energetic as he had a dozen years before.

The daktari's minibots were able to wrap her ribs and reset her broken nose. As far as her hand was concerned, there was little he could do. What bone hadn't been powdered had been reduced to splinters, some that stuck through her skin. "What did those animals do to you?" Kensey growled, no doubt referring to the Rangers.

Given time, it's possible a properly trained medic could have initiated regenerative construction to rebuild the hand from the socket up. With a squad of Rangers and an impatient squad captain literally at the examination room door, time was one element that wasn't available.

There was nothing to do but amputate her hand. Kensey whispered "samahani" to her as he applied a local anesthetic. Then, his eyes tearing, he broke out the focused-light shears. There wouldn't be time to fit her with a prosthetic graft now; it'd have to be done later, hopefully at the next infirmary she visited. Cobalt was none too happy for the delay in processing her. He'd just as soon have cut it off and tossed her into the nearest damp cell. Mercifully, we no longer lived in such dark times.

A commotion outside distracted the captain. I half-suspected Cele Dlamini was raising a fuss with him. I'd have welcomed a good night's rest, but I couldn't leave her. Not after everything we'd endured. So it was with stinging leaden irises that we perceived the arrival of Jomoro Al-Amain to take charge of us. Daktari Kensey was sparing in his conversation; doubtless the Rangers' presence set his nerves on edge as well. After a few hushed words with Jamai, Kensey ducked into the reception area. Jomoro stepped around the tropical flowered screen in his place.

"Grandfather," she wheezed, "I'm at your service."

Of all the ends we could have imagined, this scenario seemed the best of the lot. Jomoro had prepped the Rangers well. The captain deployed his troops in a double-line, forming a safe corridor leading from the clinic's rear entrance to the prison transport that waited five meters outside.

The residents of Kibarenge shuffled and glowered outside the Ranger cordon, but no one dared push past them. When Jamai and I stepped onto the clinic's gravel pathway, all sounds ceased. Even the little totos watched with mute tongues. Jamai rallied only once at the sight of her grandmother standing at the head of her aggrieved neighbors. Poor woman, her frail hands trembled over her mouth.

Keeping her bandaged wrist tight to her hip, Jamai thrust her manacled right arm in the air, shaking the cuffs as though they were bangles. "See, bibi Cele!" she grinned. "Our wedding bands."

In spite of her grief, Cele Dlamini managed a short cackle. The youngest boys joined in while her Elders, including Kadar Dlamini, appeared piqued or browbeaten. I could sympathize.

We were both going to jail; at least I would be for a short while, on a charge of assisting an escaped felon. What did we have to smile about? At least no one pitched rotten yams at us.

"They're as crazy as you are," I muttered to Jamai.

Jamai whispered back, "You're with me, so who's wearing the cocked hat now?" The fingers of her right hand slipped into mine as we stepped into the waiting transport.

Now What?

(A confidential source has released what is believed to be a portion of a diary extract to the interviewer. It has been submitted to the authorities and reproduced here with their kind permission.)

YOU SOMALI BITCH, HOW DID YOU DO THAT? How could you have swayed Ngojama to your side? The mistress herself had suggested his name to us; she said he was one of her own. You never even realized where he came from; how far, or how near either.

NOTE: in future never rely on second-hand information or heresay from such hairlips as our former agent Molefe. Well, better he is gone. It is time to reorganize our leadership positions. Best that we cast off Father Auflauring as well. As a mentor he was… diligent but too genteel, as if he could charm the Lepidopteran into serving our needs. Yes, of course the mistress is right; she always is. You'd understand, Father. I had to have Ngojama remove you.

The Lepidopteran being in police custody may be a complication. We will have to see how that situation plays out. Given the paranoia of the East African Community toward the psychically gifted and the concentration of pure power in the girl, the outcome can hardly be in doubt. That situation, however it pans, cannot be allowed. We… I… must have the shade that she possesses. My brother will receive a promotion as chief of our mistress's shepherds in our district. I pray thee patience, Mistress… Mother. I will see you free.

Cast of Players

The Dlaminis

Jamai Fatima Dlamini, the only daughter of Siboniso Dlamini, gifted with special powers; native to the village of Baba Elgonyi.

Siboniso Dlamini, her father; director for the Sahara Reclamation Project.

Fatima Nouari, her mother (deceased).

Cele Wanjiko Dlamini, Jamai's grandmother, now living with her younger son, Kadar, in the neighboring village of Kibarenge.

Kadar Dlamini, brother to Siboniso; both are sons to Cele Dlamini.

Esaias Pahoran Dlamini, Jamai's literal spiritual grandfather.

Benjamin Dlamini, Esaias' son and Jamai's ancestor 20 generations removed; founder of the village Baba Elgonyi.

The Hadebes

Youssou Hissen Hadebe, Jamai's best friend — perhaps her only friend — in Baba Elgonyi.

Ahela, his twin sister (deceased).

Lazaro and **Wanjiro Hadebe**, Youssou's father and mother.

The Molefes

Odu Molefe, the clan Elder, descendent of the oppressed Acholi people of the former state of Uganda.

Nyassa, his oldest daughter.

Hwenge and **Mutu**, his errant sons.

Kalila Maji, the youngest daughter.

The Children of Sydelle

Sydelle, a psychic girl from the mid-21st century overshadowed and physically mutated by a malevolent presence from another dimension, or sphere.

Ngojama, a beast of folklore and legend, enslaved with the brand of Sydelle; he was charged with bringing Jamai to the Children of Sydelle.

Bren Auflauring, head Master of the COS in East Africa; assassinated by Ngojama.

The Ancient Order of Elias

Elias, a well-meaning psychic of the mid-21st Century, well revered by his wards.

Li Shun Kim, a guardian of that order; assassinated by the Children of Sydelle.

Other Players

S'manga Nlebela, Jamai's physician and counselor.

Dr. Kensey, resident clinician at Kibarenge, another ally of Jamai.

Jomoro Al-Amain, District Magistrate.

Poppy Girls, basically mindless genetic constructs used for the most menial tasks.

Soldier Poppies, a more aggressive variant with genetically ingrained killer instincts.

The Rangers, the first and best defensive battalion in the East African Community.

Historical figures
(Real or Imaginary)

Sister Jamaica, a mystic widely revered in Jamai's time.

Wangari Muta Maathai, a Kenyan environmental and political activist. She founded the Green Belt movement dedicated to conservation and women's rights, and suffered arrest, assault and political pressure from the Kenyan authorities. In 2004, she won the Nobel Peace Prize for her contributions to sustainable development and democracy.

Alice Auma, aka, Alice Lakwana, an Acholi mystic who claimed to channel the spirit of a dead Italian army officer named Lakwana. She became the founder of the Holy Spirit Movement, which revolted against Uganda's President Museveni in 1986-87. She died in a Kenyan refugee camp in 2007 of unknown causes.

Joseph Kony, leader of a militant group called the Lord's Resistance Army, directly inspired by Alice Auma's Holy Spirit Movement; the LRA follows a mish-mash of Christian and animist beliefs concocted by Kony. They have fought the Ugandan government for decades and abducted 30,000 children to serve and be brutalized in their army. In October 2005, Kony and four of his associates were indicted *in abscentia* by the International Criminal Court for crimes against humanity.

Glossary

[The following words and phrases are Swahili, unless otherwise noted. All errors are unintended and solely the responsibility of the author.]

asante — thank you; *asante sana*--thank you very much

Baba — Father; for the purpose of this story, also part of the name of Jamai's home village

Bayaka — the traditional people of the Ituri forest of the Congo; also called *pygmies* in the past

bibi — Grandmother

bila shaka — (phrase) without a doubt

bwana — term of respect, meaning "sir" or "mister"

calabash — gourd, fashioned from an Old World vine of the same name

daktari — Doctor

E.A. — shorthand for the East African Community; a regional authority having little Constitutional power over its constituent parts. In some ways it is similar to the first U.S. government under the Articles of Confederation, its original constitution

eyvan — in Arabic architecture, a vast vaulted hall

fisi(s) — hyena(s)

Genocidal Wars — think about it

Habari yako — "What's your news?" Familiar Swahili greeting between close acquaintances; the traditional reply would be *mzuri sana*, "very fine"

Harmattan — (Arabic) a scouring wind coming off of the Sahara Desert

hodi! — traditional greeting, called as you approach a neighbor's home *inshallah* — (Arabic) If God wills it

jambo — standard Swahili greeting between casual acquaintances and people you are just meeting

jina lako nani? — What is your name?

kanga — a cloth wrap, bound around the waist

Kere-Nyaga — traditional name for the Masai holy mountain, Kilimanjaro

Kiama — a Council of Elders

kihoro! — "Great grief"; voice-activation code used by Jomoro Al-Amain to engage his cannon, the Adjudicator

kopje — SVU-sized boulders on the African plains

Kukuwazuka — butterfly; Youssou's pet name for Jamai

kwa nini — "Why?" or "What for?"

kwenda nyumbani — Go away

lala salama — sleep well; literally, sleep in peace

Lepidopteran — derogatory name given to Jamai not only by her age-mates but by the Children of Sydelle. Taken from the Latin, "scale-winged ones", Lepidoptera is the order of insects which includes butterflies and moths

liana — tropical climbing vines

The Lost Age — in the context of this story, the time concurrent with the Genocidal Wars where nation fought nation, and much of what transpired in that period was "lost" or forgotten

mahuti — literally "rubbish"; in this novel's context, the name given to small 'bots that collect either garbage or compost, and generally carry out small useless tasks

mama — mother; also, general term of endearment for Elderly women

matatus — Nairobi cabbies, well known for their reckless driving.

mondo-mogo — spiritual adviser

morani — a Masai warrior

morathi — a seer; *morathi wa nauma* would be a seer of darkness; Jamai's dead grandparent

Mzee — Elder or older person; term of great respect for a male.

mzuri — "fine", the response to a neighbor calling "Hodi!"

mzuri sana — "very fine"

ndiyo — yes

Ngai — the name of God; literally, Revered Elder

niache — Leave me alone!

nini — what? (see kwa nini)

nurudogo — literally, "small light"

nyoka — general term for "snake"

pembo — home-made beer

rains — the rainy seasons that come twice annually in East Africa;
the "long rains" run from April-June, while the "short
rains" are in October-December

rafiki — friend

samahani — I'm sorry

shamba(s) — cultivated field(s)

shwari — calm

siafu — ants

simba — lion

The Sudd — (Arabic for 'barrier') a 500-mile long swamp clogged
by papyrus and reeds; fed by the White Nile, it divides
Southern from Northern Sudan, culturally as well as
geographically

tafadhali — please

toto — child

uume — the...umm...penis

wuolos — African dogs

German

Der — definite article; that, the, which, who.

Fraulein — young miss

Herr — mister.

(der) junge — young man, boy, lad, hatchling.

(die) Lehrerin, or *unsere die Lehrerin* — our Mistress.

menschenfeind — misanthropist.

schwein — swine.